CORRUPT MAGIC

HIDDEN PROPHECY BOOK 4

LILY SKYY

Corrupt Magic
Copyright © 2022 by Lily Skyy
www.LilySkyy.com

First Edition: December 2022

ISBN 978-1-957989-74-7 (ebook)
ISBN 978-1-957989-75-4 (paperback)

Published by Books to Hook Publishing, LLC.
www.BooksToHook.com

CONTENTS

CHAPTER I
THE DEEP SOUTH

The flatness stretched on for miles in every direction. A sea of grass and corn stalks flowed in the late September breeze. It felt like there was not a single soul left in the world as Mitra stretched her cell phone high up toward the sun, trying to get better reception. When she glanced at it and noticed she still had no bars, she huffed in irritation.

The two-lane road was devoid of traffic but she still glanced down both directions, hoping to see some sort of sign she might have missed. It was a futile effort though, because she never missed anything. Mitra was the sort of person who noticed things others didn't; rarely did a single detail escape her attention. She had been watching for a sign for miles, trying to find the way back to the main highway. This "shortcut" was anything but short, but Haris had assured her this way was faster. He was also sure they weren't going to run out of gas, but she had a feeling she would need to be a bit more firm on that one. She had no intention of walking miles to find another gas station.

Glaring at the empty road one more time, she walked back to the green, beat-up truck parked on the shoulder and climbed into the passenger side of the cab.

"Still nothing," she said over the blaring country music, yanking the door shut. "You actually like this stuff?" she asked. She had never been a fan of the twangy sounds of acoustic love songs.

"Hm?" Haris said, looking up from the map he had pulled out of the glove box. She had picked it up at the last stop, though Haris had promised he 'knew where he was going.' "This? I like to immerse myself in my environment. Be one with my surroundings," he said mystically, with a smile. He bent back down to the map and pointed. "I'm pretty sure we are on the right track. We just need to follow this road for...a few more miles and we'll come back out to the highway. And then we should be in Tennessee tonight."

Mitra sighed, mentally preparing to walk down the highway in the dark when they got lost again and ran out of gas. "I hope so. I feel like we are wandering around in a massive corn maze."

Haris folded the map back up and tossed it in the back seat. He snorted. "That's Illinois for you," he said and put the truck back into gear before pulling onto the road again.

To Mitra's annoyance, he turned up the music.

They had only been traveling for a day and a half, even though it felt like much longer. They had left Haris's house in northern Michigan right after their friends Kinza and Zaid had gone through the portal in Haris's basement. The portal that would transport them to another portal on the other side of the planet so they could go to the magical hidden city in Tanzania.

Mitra still had a hard time remembering all that stuff was real. The last few weeks had been a nightmare for her. First, her best friend went missing and her grandmother refused to say where she was. And then she found Kinza casually walking through Chicago a week later with a man she's never seen before. And *then* Kinza told her she was the long-lost heir to a civilization of people with magical abilities and she had to go live in that hidden city for the rest of her life as their queen. If Mitra was being honest with herself, it still hadn't set in yet, that she wouldn't see her best friend ever again. In her mind, she would wake up tomorrow and they would both go to work, cleaning toilets for the fancy businesses in downtown Chicago.

Yet here she was, hunting a deranged monster with magic powers across the country with a sometimes equally deranged red-haired guy she met a few days ago. Seriously, was he ever in a bad mood? Mitra didn't understand how he could be so cheerful all the time.

She glanced over at Haris in the driver's seat. A pair of sunglasses sat over his eyes and his fingers tapped against the steering wheel out of time with the music. She didn't know how she felt about him yet. He had flirted with her relentlessly since they met at Kinza's house a few days ago, but he seemed to have a similar disposition with everyone. He was always teasing or grinning, cracking jokes at the worst times. She could have sworn he did it more with her, though...

Haris caught her looking and waggled his eyebrows over his glasses. "Want to take a picture? It'll last longer." Point in case.

Mitra crossed her arms and turned back to the road without answering, thankful she also had on a pair of gigantic sunglasses that partially hid her blush. She refused to be embarrassed though; she just was not that type of girl.

Literally nothing made him mad either. Mitra had tried for the first day, taking over the crackly stereo and pumping her most obnoxious songs through the speakers. Haris only bobbed his head along with the noise. She even went so far as to start backseat driving, telling him to slow down or use his blinker or speed up, but he only remarked on how *helpful* she was being. Maybe he had been sarcastic. Either way, she gave up on trying to push his buttons pretty quickly seeing as it had little effect on him. They had a job to focus on, anyway.

Kinza and Zaid had filled her in on the ubir that they were chasing. Apparently the Anunnaki—Kinza's people—weren't supposed to just leave their city, or they would lose their memories and powers. A group of rebellious Anunnaki discovered a way to leave while keeping their powers, but it required routine blood sacrifices and warped their minds over time. They turned into something very close to a monster from a children's nightmare, stealing people in the night. Similar to a drug addiction, the longer they practiced this ritual, the more broken their minds became, until they were killing people for pleasure.

The ubir normally moved throughout the world alone, but they would occasionally form small groups of twos or threes and cause that much more damage for the venari—the Anunnaki bounty hunters—to clean up. Kinza and Zaid had run into one of these packs a few weeks ago, killing two of them, but the third escaped. Basma was her name, and she was supposed to have some sort of agility power, like a zombie gymnast. Kinza had described her as more aware than the others. Maybe she had been practicing the blood rituals for less time. Either way, they couldn't let her go free, so Haris had offered to track her down for Zaid.

Mitra had immediately demanded to come along, but she wasn't ready to admit to herself why yet. Instead, she thought about how it had been a thousand times more boring than she expected monster-hunting to be.

"Remind me why we just couldn't have used the portal at

your house to pop down to one of the others down south instead of driving the whole way?" she asked. The windows were cracked; the further south they got, the warmer it was and Mitra was relishing the breeze whipping over her long braid.

"We aren't allowed to," Haris replied brightly. She could tell he didn't like that fact based on the slightly pained smile. "They're only for Anunnaki; venari specifically. No humans allowed."

"So you guard over the portal your whole life. You operate it so the venari can use it. And you keep it hidden from other humans. Yet Ummanu can't use it?" She was a bit skeptical of the rules between the Anunnaki and their Ummanu allies.

"Pretty much," Haris said. "But in all honesty, we don't really travel much. What we're doing right now is pretty unconventional. Ummanu don't keep tabs on ubir, let alone track them down. We have a few things to protect ourselves, but we try to keep off their radar. Which is what makes this so exciting!"

Mitra secretly had to agree. Despite the endless fields of corn and wheat, the thought of tracking down a rabid Anunnaki had her energized in a way she hadn't been in a long time. There was nothing in her life that had her springing out of bed in the morning as much as this.

Haris had started singing along to the music, and not quietly.

"Do you want me to drive?" Mitra asked.

"Not a chance!" Haris sang and kept on driving. "Either way, we shouldn't be far now. Look up where the motel is again on the map."

"Why do we have to stay in a grimy motel?" Mitra said, reaching into the backseat for the map.

"Do I look like I'm made of money to you?" he asked,

making a face behind his glasses. "Portal-guarding doesn't exactly pay much. Nothing, in fact. I still have to have a human job to pay the bills."

"You do all that for free?" Mitra asked. She couldn't find anything on the map so she pulled out her phone. Still no reception.

"Yup. I'm a good Samaritan," Haris said, running a hand over his hair.

Mitra checked her phone again and yelped. "I've got reception!" She quickly looked up their location and how far it was to the motel. Haris was off by a few hours, though. She gave him the directions and took a screenshot of them, just in case.

"I think we should go over the evidence again," Mitra said, putting her phone away.

"Well, there isn't much," Haris said. "We know Linda said there was a body found by the local police a few miles outside of Jackson. They said the blood was drained and looked a bit ritualistic, which tends to be the ubir's trademark. But that was days ago. I got another hit from an Ummanu named Abe down in Louisiana, something about more murders that way, too."

"I'm guessing we'll stop and check them both out if we don't find Basma here?" Mitra asked as they flew down the highway.

"Might as well."

"What do we do when we find her?"

Haris turned to her with a devilish grin. "Do you know how to fight?"

Mitra snorted and looked out the window, but deep down she could feel that thrum of excitement building.

"Sorry kids, that's all I got."

Mitra and Haris stood dejectedly on Linda's white-painted porch. The two-story house sat in a picture-perfect suburban neighborhood in Memphis that looked like it could have come out of a magazine. The potted plants on her doorstep were immaculate and her two kids played in the yard while mommy had a "business meeting."

The woman herself looked nothing short of a typical soccer mom. Short blond hair, expensive athleisure, and one eye on her kids at all times. Mitra was a little baffled that this woman had connections to the Anunnaki and even knew what the ubir were. She looked like she was about to attend the local PTA meeting after they were done before proceeding to the town bake sale, where she would present her "famous" snicker-doodle cookies just like last year. She didn't have time to ogle at the pretty house or smell what was baking in the oven before Linda had jumped into her story about the murders.

They had spent the night in the grimy motel Mitra had detested and gotten up early to get a head start, making it into town by late morning. Linda had invited them in and offered them sweet tea and some lemon bars, which Haris accepted enthusiastically. She had gone over the murder that had happened five days ago now, but it was just as Haris described. A ritualistic murder of a young woman outside of Jackson. The body was found on the train tracks with the throat and wrists slit; something she couldn't have done herself. The police had found little signs of struggle and no suspects whatsoever.

When it was clear that Linda wouldn't have any other helpful information, Mitra took the opportunity to drill the woman with questions about being Ummanu in plain sight, what her life was like, or if any of her family knew. Mitra wanted to take every opportunity to ask about the people who lived this lifestyle before she went back to her boring life with strict rules and expectations. She answered patiently and when she had gone to check on her kids, Haris elbowed her.

"This isn't an interrogation. I can tell you anything you want to know about being Ummanu," he said.

"I'm just curious," she replied. Mitra had always been a curious child and a thorough student, to her parents' delight. She just wanted to know *more.* "A week ago, none of this stuff existed for me."

They had taken their leave, saying goodbye to Linda with a promise from Haris to connect more in the future.

"Well, now what?" Mitra said while jumping into the driver's seat. Haris didn't complain, only tossing her the keys.

"Just start driving," he said. "I'll see if I can give Abe a call."

Mitra navigated through busy Memphis and out to the highway again, headed south. Haris had a conversation with the man named Abe, yet he had an odd expression the entire time and asked the man to repeat himself more than once.

"That was fun," Haris said, ending the call.

"What?"

"That's the thickest accent I've ever heard. He said they had two murders down that way, similar to the one Linda described. The last one was two days ago, though. I still think it's worth checking out." Haris leaned his head on the back of the seat, drumming his fingers on the door.

"Alright, Louisiana it is." It was quiet for a moment before Mitra asked, "So, how *did* you get into this stuff?"

Haris rolled his head to look at her, brown eyes questioning.

"You said you would tell me whatever I wanted to know," she reminded him.

"Ah, right. Well, I—" he hesitated as if thinking "—was chosen on a game show as a child," he said with a totally straight face. "Something about my look screamed 'defender of portals, hunter of monsters, most attractive dude alive.' Or something like that." He finally flashed her one of those grins of his.

Mitra shook her head, trying not to laugh. She had spent her fair share around guys, having a string of boyfriends in high school that all wanted to impress her with their shiny cars, fancy clothes, and stoic demeanor. She couldn't help but compare Haris to the other guys she's known, so she felt like she was stuck in a group project with the class jokester.

"Ha, ha, so you just happened to have your career chosen for you as a child. Must be rough."

"Yep," Haris said, leaning his seat back and placing his hand behind his head. "Unlike you. The world is your oyster."

"If only," Mitra grumbled to herself. She would've given anything to have the kind of freedom he did. Everything had been chosen for her since she was a child. Her parents pushed her career options, her extracurriculars, and even certain boys in her direction. They loved her dearly, but sometimes their love could be suffocating. She had managed to get them to let her take a year off before college, citing that all the wealthy kids did it. But in reality, she just wanted more time. More time before she had to start working toward a career and a life she didn't want. Every day, she dreaded having to fill out college applications to the nation's best medical schools while fending off her mother's constant prodding for her to go on a date with a friend's "perfect" son.

She didn't have to think about that right now, though. With the blue sky above her and the beat-up truck beneath her, she turned up the volume and let the obnoxious music Haris had chosen wash over her as they headed to the deep south of Louisiana.

THEY CHOSE to stay one more night in a motel, to Mitra's disgust. She could have sworn the bed had bugs, so she wrapped herself in a towel before laying on the floor to sleep. Haris had no such qualms and was tucked beneath the blankets on his bed and asleep within minutes.

Mitra had a hard time falling asleep, so she scrolled through her phone, looking at social media, the news, and old pictures of her and Kinza. She wondered what her friend was doing at that moment. Was she safely back in that magical city of hers, or was she hunting monsters just like Mitra? They had seen each other almost every day for years, so she had felt bereft this last week without her. It seemed that Kinza had her life all figured out now and Mitra was approaching...nothing.

As she did every night, Mitra sent a text to Kinza, knowing that she wouldn't receive it unless she left the city—no reception in magical lands. She told her how her day was and what she and Haris were up to. She suggested that the two of them take a real road trip sometime soon, knowing that it would never happen.

Mitra wiped a tear that had slipped out of the corner of her eye before shutting her phone off and attempting to sleep. Just before she drifted off, she had the rebellious thought that maybe that was why she wanted to come with Haris. While she was off monster hunting with him, it felt like she was still part of Kinza's world, and the moment it ended, her best friend would be beyond her reach.

It DIDN'T TAKE them long the next morning to get down to Thibodaux. Abe lived just a few miles from there, seemingly out in the middle of nowhere. Mitra couldn't get over how humid it was, even in September. She was glad they had stopped to get clothes at a random store, but the t-shirt and cutoff shorts she had on still felt like a parka.

They drove down a single-lane county road further south, following the directions Abe had given them. Apparently, he had his own plot of land out here where the portal was. The further they got, the more trees and water they found. Houses and buildings disappeared behind them and they finally found the mark on the side of the road where the driveway was. It went on for another quarter mile through the trees; the truck bouncing along on the uneven road.

They pulled up to what Mitra thought was a literal junkyard.

"Are you sure this is it?" she asked.

Haris slowed the truck down, peering out the windshield. "Um, not really..."

They looked around a lot filled with various old cars, tires, scrap material, a bathtub, and even a school bus. There were also scattered children's toys, piles of wood, dog crates, the three dogs themselves, and a broken kiddie pool. Mitra finally spotted the house beneath a curtain of wind chimes and wind fans. The single-story shack was actually relatively decent in size, if you actually made it to the door without tripping and harming yourself.

The dogs had little interest as Haris pulled up as far as he could and killed the engine. On the side of the makeshift driveway was an old sign that said "NO TRESPASSING."

"Maybe we should call again..." Mitra suggested as they got out and walked up to the door.

"I think it's a little late for that," Haris replied. There was a large porch across the front of the house, and it looked like the short staircase had fallen in long ago, replaced by a few cinder blocks. There was no way the owner would hear them coming with the army of wind chimes blowing, but they went up and knocked on the screen door.

At first, there was no answer, so Haris knocked again, harder this time. They heard movement from within and saw a shadow on the other side of the frosted glass of the inner door. The thumping of footsteps grew louder just as the shadow loomed on the other side of the door.

After what felt like a year, the door opened and on the other side of the screen, Mitra saw exactly what she had dreaded. An older man stood there, a little taller than herself, but three times as wide. Wild tufts of gray hair stuck out from underneath the straw hat, and she caught a glimpse of several missing teeth in the angry face of the man as he pushed open the screen door.

Mitra waited for him to yell at them for trespassing.

Then, in the thickest southern accent she had ever heard, "What took y'all so long?!"

CHAPTER 2
DARK VISIONS

Thick, wet leaves slapped Eta's face as she stumbled through the forest. Roots rose up to grab her, and she fell in a heap. Her heart thundered in her chest as she looked over her shoulder, but she couldn't remember what she was running from. Looking at her hands and feet, she realized the leaves weren't red with rainwater, but with blood. Frantically trying to wipe them off, she got to her feet and started running again.

Between one tree and the next, everything changed. She was in a dark valley; the sun hidden behind the mountains. It was barren and the sharp rocks bit into her feet. She took a step and found herself strapped to a metal table, lights glaring down from above. Shadows moved, whispering in corners as she struggled against the straps.

"Help!" she called.

"Eta?" a voice said in the darkness. She recognized the voice but couldn't think of their face. How had she gotten here? What was happening? She jerked as hard as she could and this time, she flipped off the table and fell into deep water. It was even darker in here and she thrashed to get to the surface. Bright sunlight twinkled *above and she gasped as she broke the surface, only to find the sunlight gone, hidden behind the trees.*

She was in a murky swamp, trees closing in around her. She started to swim to shore but something about the water looked wrong. She angled herself to get a look in better light, but wished she hadn't.

It was blood. She swam in blood and it cascaded in rivulets down her face. Eta screamed for help, for anything. She didn't know how she got here and wanted desperately to leave.

"Help! Help!"

"Eta!" the voice called again. She called even louder so they could find her.

"Please! Somebody find me!"

"Eta!" The sound came much closer now and Eta's eyes flew open to see the panicked face of Mikah in front of her, gripping her shoulders like he was the one drowning. Upon seeing her awake, he let out a long sigh and fell back into a chair, and rubbed his face.

What in the name of the Creator was that? he asked into her mind.

Eta looked around to see they were in her office in the Grand Hall, in the great city of Rhapta. Her desk sat by the window like it always did, with the bookshelves across the room. She and Mikah were seated in chairs in the middle, with stacks of paper all around them. There was no swamp in sight and definitely no blood.

Oh, right. They had been in the middle of going over recent reports when she had fallen into a vision. Looking down at herself, she realized she was soaked through with sweat. Wiping the arms of her gray robes over her face, she said, *A vision. The first big one I've had since...*

Since the one in the quarries, Mikah supplied.

She nodded, even though he already knew the answer. The city had been rife with changes since Kinza's coronation just two days ago, and she was surprised she hadn't had another vision of this caliber in that time. They had recently narrowly avoided being found by humans when the ex-Elder Tahir had led them to Rhapta's door with a literal army. Thankfully, Kinza had found a way to keep them hidden and Tahir out, so the army had dwindled back down Mount Kilimanjaro, where Rhapta sat.

They had still been on high alert since.

Tell me about it? Mikah asked, standing to get her a glass of water. Their relationship had developed into something different over the last week or two. They were more than just friends, but less than...she couldn't think about that right now.

There was blood. A lot of it, she said. *A forest, a valley. I was strapped to a table with bright lights and whispering shadows.*

Joyful, Mikah said with a grimace, handing her the water. She gulped it down in seconds and Mikah went to refill it for her.

It was surely ominous, she said, trying to remember the little details like her old mentor Hakim had taught her to do. *Something is going to happen. Something bad.*

Mikah returned with the water and she sipped it slower this time. *Anything in particular? A date? A location? A motive?*

She shook her head. *It was just...dark.* She leaned back, her heart had calmed and the sweat or something else made her shiver. *I suppose we just have to wait for another one. There's nothing we can do about it now. Thank you, by the way. It's never enjoyable coming out of it.*

Mikah waved her off. *It's nothing,* he said with another sigh, rubbing at his temples. He had been doing that all morning. Eta had mixed feelings about it. She knew that this distress he was feeling was something no one else got to see. She was slowly growing accustomed to how he dropped his ever-charming façade the moment they were alone. While she felt a small bit of pride that he trusted her enough to do so, she didn't actually enjoy seeing him like this. And it was something more than her vision.

What's wrong? she asked, shifting the papers she had on her lap; reports on total deaths in the city over the last few weeks. Maybe that was what had triggered the vision.

Mikah eyed her from his seat. *Did you see that in your vision? That something was wrong?*

No. You've just looked...glum all morning. Did something happen that I should have seen? she asked.

He seemed to relax a little. *No,* he paused before continuing, *my father is just putting his usual pressure on me. He is not pleased with my actions lately.*

What do you mean? As an Advisor to the queen? Mikah and the rest of the Advisors had put in just as much, if not more work than anyone else these past days. What was there to be displeased about?

Mikah traced circles over the armrest of the chair, thinking. *My father is...a strict man. He has very rigid views of what I should be doing with my life and being Advisor to the queen is not one of them.*

What? Eta said. *How could he be any less proud? There is no higher position in the city other than the queen. Would he prefer you were still Tahir's Apprentice?*

The confirming look he gave her made Eta's mouth pop open. *You can't be serious. Anyone who would prefer that Tahir was in power is someone whose head was not screwed on straight.* She felt an unusual wave of anger bubble up, but she took steadying breaths to push it back down.

Mikah shrugged. *My father has always been a man of the old ways. He always wants things to be just perfect—at least in his eyes. Did you know his ability is to repair things that are broken? He can fix small things, making them whole again.*

Hmm, I feel like there is something interesting behind that. Well, don't let him stress you out. We have too much going on for you to be sparing a single thought toward something like that. Speaking of which, she said as she glanced toward the clock, *we have a meeting in an hour. I need to clean up, so I'll meet you there?*

Mikah nodded.

Feel free to stay here if you want; this office is half yours anyway, she said and went to go soak in a bathtub for the next forty-five minutes. She still felt the memory of the blood running down her face and shuddered as she closed the door behind her.

MIKAH WATCHED ETA LEAVE, gripping the armrest of the chair. He hated that he was glad she left. Not that he wanted her to leave, per se, but that he didn't want her to dig. He hadn't lied when he told her about his father, but he underplayed it quite a bit.

The night before, he had been summoned by his father for an after-dinner discussion. Mikah had to listen to nearly an hour-long ramble about how far he had fallen in such a short time. It was his father who had pushed him into the apprenticeship with Tahir, citing that the closer they were to the man, the more they would be in power. It was never said outright, but Mikah's father had found out it was he who had stopped Tahir from killing Kinza. It would be something close to treason to speak out against that act, but his father had gotten dangerously close.

Instead, he had thrown scalding words at Mikah about

how pathetic he was for accepting an Advisor position instead of attempting to swoon the new queen into marriage. Mikah had to suppress an eye-roll. *If only he knew.* Throughout that hour, he was expected to stand there and receive a verbal lashing for all of his supposed wrongdoings without even flinching. At the end of the meeting, his father had detailed a long and ridiculous plan to seduce the queen and take over as consort in the future so that Mikah's father could all but rule through him. He was instructed to return in a few days with his first steps completed.

He stood and walked over to the window that overlooked the back gardens. A gardener must have come by because they were in full bloom despite being torn up just a few weeks ago.

Mikah wanted to tell him his plan was just another version of treason, but he knew his father would only counter that it wasn't treason if they weren't killing the queen. Only influencing her.

He had no intentions of doing a single thing his father said. He still had to deal with the man's wrath when he found out, though. Would his father cut contact with him? He didn't actually need the man for support. Mikah got everything he needed through the Grand Hall, but cutting one's parents out of their life was no easy feat.

He ran a finger down the glass, watching two people walk up the path, recognizing them as they got close. It was Kinza and Zaid, the latter barely suppressing a grin at something the former said. Mikah noticed they always walked close enough so their hands were constantly brushing, as if they never wanted to part from each other. Kinza had practically declared to the world that Zaid was with her and there wouldn't be a single discussion about it, despite grumblings about how he didn't come from the proper background for a queen. Mikah wanted to bottle that conviction and show his father that his plan was nothing short of ridiculous. As far as Kinza was concerned, Zaid was the only man on the entire planet.

They moved out of sight, probably up to the meeting room. Mikah still had some time before he had to leave, so he wandered around the office, looking over Eta's books and notes. She kept endless logs of her visions, some of them nothing more than gibberish. They were scrawled in the margins of books like she had written them down in the moment, or neatly laid out on a sheet as if having pondered them for days.

She was right, though: he had practically moved himself into her office, his things scattered about the room. Reports that he had to complete, proposals that needed to be approved, and a mug of his tea on the shelf. Being around her was a relief. He couldn't relax like that around anyone else. What use was it hiding from a seer? She had seen through him from the first day they met. She had scorned him at first when he was still beneath Tahir's wing. Yet, she accepted his help later when she realized he was sincere. There was nothing he could keep from her, so the mask he wore around everyone else seemed to slip off when they were alone.

Here he was, though, trying to hide his oldest pains from her so she wouldn't feel pity for him. He knew she would find out eventually how terrible his father was, but he rued the day she looked at him like a poor, beaten child.

Running a hand over his face, he glanced at the clock. There was no use twiddling his thumbs in here, so Mikah melted into the version of himself that most people saw and left Eta's office.

ETA KNOCKED BEFORE STEPPING into Kinza's makeshift office. She had spent as long as possible lounging in the warm bath water, letting it soak away the terror of the vision. She tried not to think about all the blood as it cooled, but thoughts of the vision kept coming back, albeit quieter.

Kinza, Zaid, and Mikah were already there along with Advisors Ekbal, Badr, Ishar, and Balasi.

Looks like I am the last one, she said as she closed the door and took a seat. Kinza sat behind her desk, curls piled on top of her head today, making her look more regal than normal. Zaid stood as close as physically possible without touching her.

Let's begin then, Kinza said, tossing a slice of orange in the air before catching it in her mouth. So much for regal. *We have a lot to discuss, and only an hour to do it. Ekbal, would you like to go first?*

The older man nodded. *I do have a bit of good news. Despite all the havoc that has been going on these past few weeks, the crop yield is turning out spectacularly well. We did, unfortunately, have quite a few deaths among those who work the fields, so we'll need to keep an eye out for future pupils with relative abilities. But otherwise, we'll have more than enough food to last us through the dry season.*

Good, Kinza said with a nod. *We don't want people to starve. Ishar, anything new?*

Ishar nodded, his bushy white eyebrows furrowing in concentration. *Yes, I've been working with Savar,* he said with a nod to Zaid, *on the state of the venari. As usual, numbers are extremely low and ubir numbers are always higher. Even higher with recent events. But Savar mentioned he is coming up with a plan for the near future; something about getting new recruits.*

Zaid's brows lowered at that. It seemed as though this was the first time the brooding venari had heard this. Eta had gathered that Zaid was close with the head of the venari, but everyone had their secrets.

Okay, great, Kinza said. *Badr? Anything?*

Badr jumped up from his seat at his name. Out of all of them here, Eta had noticed the new position had only increased Badr's energy instead of decreasing it. He was able to truly work in his element in his new position of Advisor *and* official scholar to the queen—something he liked to brag about even though he was still considered an Apprentice within the scholars themselves.

We're making progress on the ink used in our tattoos. I think it'll still take some time to get the formula right, but we are on track to completing it so we can leave the city in the near future, he said quickly.

How near? Zaid asked, crossing his arms.

Realistically? A year or so, Badr said. *I'm confident we'll get the formula right long before then, but we have to find a way to repeat it in high doses. The good news is that we are headed in the right direction now that we know it's possible.*

Kinza popped another slice of orange in her mouth before saying, *Okay, I consider that a win. Regardless, neither the Anunnaki nor the human race is ready for us to reenter the world yet, so we have some time. Thank you, Badr. Mikah? Balasi?*

Eta and I are still going through the mountain of old reports, trying to stay on top of the paperwork for you, Mikah said.

Kinza gave them a sheepish smile. *And I appreciate you both endlessly for it. Keep at it! Balasi?*

The quiet, former Elder hesitated before speaking, every word always calculated. *I'll be honest, it's difficult right now to keep tabs on what is going on in the human world. I know we have venari out there and our Ummanu allies, but with the human-Anunnaki in France and China no longer on our side, we are in the dark a bit. All Ummanu in those areas are a bit quieter as well. This is why we are having a hard time "seeing" beyond the walls, if you understand my meaning.*

Kinza sighed, dropping the rest of the orange on her desk. Eta knew she felt the burden of only having one human-Anunnaki allied with them. Kinza acted as if it were her fault when she was only picking up the pieces of a broken political system. Eta caught Zaid looking at the queen with heavy concern and knew she was right.

Okay, we'll come up with a plan to get more eyes and ears out in human society. For now, let's table it. Anything else anyone wants to share? Kinza asked, looking around the room.

It was quiet for a moment before Mikah cleared his throat, looking at Eta. She pursed her lips, not wanting to talk about it.

I suppose I can share one thing, but it's rather vague, Eta said reluctantly.

Another vision? Badr asked, curiously.

Eta nodded and they all fixed their eyes on her intently. She didn't actually blame them. The last time she had a big vision, she discovered where the Anunnaki originated from as well as several possible futures for their race. It was no small revelation.

It's not good. I have a feeling something bad is going to happen, but I'm not sure what. The vision was of blood, a forest, a valley, a swamp, and I was strapped to a table. I'm not sure how any of those are connected, or even if they are at all, but it left me with a bad feeling, Eta said, looking down at her hands.

I'd say so, Ishar huffed. Everyone had gone slightly pale. *Should we be keeping an eye out for Tahir again?* he said, looking toward the queen.

I don't think so, Eta replied. *I didn't get the impression it had anything to do with the city.*

It could very well be something outside the city, out in the human world, Balasi said darkly. *Since I don't have a lot of infor-*

mation coming in, anything could be happening. I'll try to dig deeper. I don't want any more surprises knocking at our door.

Kinza nodded grimly.

The rest of the meeting passed with a sense of anxiety in the room; updates about repairs still being made after the attack on the city and the rebuilding of certain sectors. Eta tuned most of it out, constantly checking her fingernails, expecting to find blood crusted underneath. Hakim would have told her not to worry about the vision since it didn't tell her much, therefore there wasn't much she could do about it. Yet she still worried. What if someone died and it was her fault for not figuring it out? What if something did happen to the city again? Rhapta had gone through so much in the past few weeks, she didn't know how much more they could bear.

As the meeting ended, she caught Mikah and told him she was going to be done for the day. She needed a good night's rest before she could tackle the mounds of work in her office again.

CHAPTER 3
INTO THE BAYOU

Haris and Mitra sat at Abe's kitchen table. Well, it was a couple of card tables duct-taped together, but Haris supposed you could eat an omelet here all the same. Thankfully, the scary man that had answered the door had been anything but. He had ushered the two of them inside, asking if they wanted any fresh-pressed orange juice. Mitra had declined, but Haris wasn't about to pass up on free OJ. So here they sat, while Abe went into the other room to collect the report he had about the murders.

"Does it smell funny to you in here?" Mitra asked, looking around.

"Probably ran out of scented candles. You could offer to pick some up for him," Haris offered. It was probably the fact that there was no A/C and the temp outside had been sweltering, even in late September. He missed his little cottage up near the shore of Lake Michigan with the quiet buzz of the inn.

Haris spent most of his time alone, other than the occasional venari that came through his portal. He spent his days being a gardener for the inn and went home to an empty house in the evenings. It was terribly lonely so, body odor or not, he wouldn't complain about the company he had right now. Having someone by his side every second of the day for the past few days had been something new for him. It wasn't a bad feeling; he just felt like he was no longer having conversations with himself anymore. He wondered if the feeling would wear off or if it would stay.

Abe ambled back into the kitchen, deftly avoiding the stack of cardboard boxes in the corner as if it had always been there.

"Here ya go," he said, handing Haris a crumpled piece of paper. "These are the dates and locations of the murders. All the same. Neck and wrists slashed and bodies drained of blood. Both found on the other side of town."

Haris looked over the paper. There wasn't a lot of information here. "Did anyone see anything? Suspects at all?"

Abe shook his head and scratched his chest. "Not really. Only one person mentioned seeing a woman with that first fella two nights ago behind a gas station, but that was hours before he was dead. No witnesses on the other one. Both of them were...not doing well in life, if you know what I mean. Wouldn't be missed," he said, arching one caterpillar brow.

"Alright, maybe we should check it out," Haris said, looking at Mitra. He was surprised at how well she was taking all of this, half expecting her to flip out at any new piece of evidence. Instead, she was nodding her head vigorously.

"You both Ummanu from where again?" Abe asked.

"Yes, I have a portal up in northern Michigan, and this is my...consultant from Chicago," Haris said, grinning at the thought of giving Mitra an official title. It was so formal.

Abe let out a low whistle. "Y'all came a long way. I should tell ya that I already went over to both places, just in case. Don't want any of them ubir knocking on my door, right? But I didn't find anything at all. I brought a Deathstone too, to see if anyone nearby reacted, but nothing. Not a peep."

"So we don't really even know if it was an ubir that was here?" Haris thought out loud. Sure, ritualistic killings were a sign of ubir, but that also wasn't something humans haven't done before either. Could have easily been a local serial killer. Haris thought over all the other ubir he had seen in his life and their patterns. Most of them were pretty easy to spot if you knew what you were looking for, but he had never been on a hunt for one before.

He tried to think over what his mother would do. She was always a very pragmatic woman, telling him not to worry about what he can't do but to do what he could do.

"Boy, I've been doing this a lot longer than you," Abe said, leaning against the kitchen counter. "I didn't see her, and there ain't a lot of evidence, but I know something is up in my town. It's ubir, I can smell it."

"They have a smell?" Mitra asked, and Haris coughed to suppress his laugh.

"I suppose they aren't big on hygiene," he said.

Abe laughed at that. "That's true. Most of them are the dirtiest people I've seen, and trust me, I've seen some dirty people."

"So, you've been doing this your whole life?" Mitra asked Abe curiously.

"Yes, ma'am," said Abe. "My parents were Ummanu, and two of my grandparents. The portal out back has been in my family for generations now."

"Wow," she replied. "So you've seen a lot of the Anunnaki then?" Haris didn't stop her questions this time. He knew she was hungry for information, and he couldn't imagine what life would have been like had he been a normal human. Would he have gone to public school and had lots of friends? Would he have gone to college? He couldn't even picture himself putting on a suit and working in an office. The thought made him smile.

"The venari, yes, seen tons of them. Some of them several times over. Most of them stick to one region of the world," Abe said. "I once met a woman who could walk on walls!"

"That's crazy," Mitra said, with wonder in her eyes. "Have you ever been to Rhapta?"

Abe bellowed out a laugh that had the dogs running in from outside. He had to shoo them back out before responding. "No way, we ain't allowed there. Ummanu stay put and let the venari through so they can do their jobs. It's a fragile ecosystem." Abe eyed her over. "How exactly are you a consultant? I see you don't know much about being Ummanu."

Mitra glanced at Haris, and he just shrugged. No point in lying.

"I have ties to the new queen," she said, casually looking at Abe.

"Ah, yes. I heard they had a new ruler over there. Little lady, big powers. Something like that. I wonder how things are going to change," Abe wondered.

"Oh, Kinza is amazing. Things will probably change for the better. She wants to help everyone. Maybe Ummanu could even travel the portals one day," Mitra replied.

Abe's eyebrows rose. "How you know all that?"

"Well." Mitra looked like she realized she would have to spill. "Kinza is my best friend. She's from Chicago too."

Abe's jaw dropped. He slapped his thigh. "Well dang, girl! You really picked a good one, didn't ya!" He laughed again, shaking his head.

"Yeah," Mitra said with a half-grin. Haris wondered if she was missing her friend right about now. "Although I didn't know anything about the Ummanu until recently. There is so much more to it than I thought. It's almost like being a secret detective," she mused.

Abe snapped his fingers. "I'm glad you mentioned that. I have some connections to the local police department. An ol' buddy of mine helped me out with an ubir problem ten years back and he's kept this whole thing hush-hush. I can give 'em a call and see if anything new has come up? They get all the gossip before it's released on the news."

"That would be very helpful, thank you," Haris said.

"Well, if the ubir is here, it's my problem, too," Abe said. "Give me a few and I'll give Larry a call." He ambled back out of the room to the back of the house. Maybe his phone still had a cord?

Haris was impressed. He didn't have those kinds of ties up in Michigan. His town didn't see a lot of ubir and risking telling the humans about the Anunnaki was too great.

Haris and Mitra looked at each other, thinking the same thing. They weren't doing too well on this hunt, and if Basma got away, that would be bad. He would hate to have to call Zaid and tell him he lost the ubir. There had to be a way to find her.

Abe wasn't gone two minutes before he hurried back in. "You two got time? Larry said he hasn't seen anyone looking like ubir, but there is something he wanted to talk to ya'll about. He'll be here in twenty."

"Sure, we can wait," Mitra said.

"Great!" Abe said. "I'll make lunch while we wait." He lifted a dead fish that had been thawing in the sink, and Haris couldn't contain the laugh at Mitra's look of horror.

Twenty-five minutes later, the kitchen was now becoming crowded with the addition of Abe's three dogs that had come in due to the cooking fish, and Larry, the police officer. He was a rather non-descript man in his middling years with a slight belly and a slow gait. He smiled brightly at Haris and Mitra though, more than happy they were there.

"So, Abe here's already filled you in on what's been going on, right?" Larry asked, rubbing the head of one of the dogs. Haris had one sitting between his knees as well, demanding a back rub.

"Yeah, he mentioned a couple of murders that might be connected to the ubir we're hunting," Mitra said.

"Well, I got something for ya, but I'm not sure it's your ubir," Larry said. "We've had more than five people go missing and have found four dead over the last six months. All about one town over. The bodies were found down in the bayou in the water, so it was difficult to get much off of them, but there's definitely something going on."

"That's well over what the normal ubir would kill in that time period. Nine people? Geez," Haris said.

"That's what I was thinking," Abe said as he tended to the sizzling fish on the stove. It only added to the boiling heat in the kitchen, but the big man hardly seemed to notice.

"How did they die?" Mitra asked.

Larry shrugged. "The four we found all died in a variety of ways. The problem is all but one was found *in* the water, so their bodies were too distorted and swollen to really get a good autopsy. The fourth died by asphyxiation."

"Hmm, not normally indicative of ubir. I'm not sure how that relates to Basma. Maybe she joined another pack," Haris thought.

"That or we lost her altogether," Mitra said, looking at him, brown eyes doubtful. "These deaths sound more like a local gang or a serial killer on a binge. Do ubir normally keep humans captive?"

Abe shook his head. "Not much. Just long enough to kill 'em, and then the body turns up soon after."

"I would mighty appreciate it if you had a chance to look into it," Larry said after a few minutes of silence. "We've got absolutely nothing, and the public is hounding us for results. Even just give it a try."

Haris thought it over, rubbing at his jaw. It was apparent that there was nothing they could do about Basma for the time being, and Larry needed help with an issue that could potentially be more ubir.

"It wouldn't be a terrible idea to hang around for a few days. We could check out what's going on in your town while waiting for Basma to make a move," he said finally. Mitra nodded along with him. He wondered why she was so eager to do this.

Larry wrote down the information on the location of the four recent murders in his town. They were all located off of a remote stretch of road that wound south, down near a large area of uninhabited forest, bayou, and marshland. The road skirted the edge of it and meandered back north. Larry told them there were a few houses and docks out that way for people who practically lived on the water or went fishing, but it was pretty devoid of people. It would make a great place to drop a body.

The four of them ate lunch at Abe's and then Mitra and Haris left to go look for clues, promising to call if anything came up.

"So, what do you think happened to those nine people?" Mitra asked. She was driving this time, one hand dangling out the window as Haris gave her directions. "I feel like we would have better luck checking out the two deaths Abe mentioned. Those sound much more like ubir to me."

Haris looked up from the passenger seat. "Are you an expert on ubir habits now?" he asked with a half-smile. When Mitra only rolled her eyes, he said, "Honestly, I'm not sure. I've never done this before and usually I find ubir when they are too close to me and my portal. At that point, I usually run and hide until a venari catches them. I'm not the one normally hunting them. I think you're right, though; the four deaths and five missing people sound more like a local human problem instead of an ubir one."

Mitra tried to think through all the crime shows she watched obsessively. After the detectives were presented with a clue, they usually just followed the trail until they found the perpetrator. But what kinds of clues did an ubir leave behind? "What are we supposed to be looking for?" Mitra asked out loud.

Haris was still looking at the map, one fist propped against his face while he leaned on the center console. "I'm not sure. Blood?" he guessed.

Mitra shivered. "I hope not."

It took them twenty-five minutes to get to the stretch of road Larry had marked and the afternoon heat had them sweating profusely the entire way. Looking at where they were headed, Mitra could see why the bodies were dumped around here. The neighborhoods slowly trickled away, and the trees were packed closer to the road as they got further south. She could see a multitude of lakes, swamps, and waterways on either side of the road, and land was becoming scarcer the more they drove.

Mitra pulled over on a stretch of road with more trees looming on either side and she could see a waterway behind the trees off to her left. From here, the road turned west and eventually would head back north; they were as south as they could get.

"This is it," Haris said, looking around and glancing at the map again. "Larry said all four bodies were found along this waterway on the left. Three were actually in the water, and one in the trees."

"Let's check it out then," Mitra said, killing the engine and hopping out. She heard Haris get out too, so she wandered over to the tree line. The air immediately felt more oppressive, like she was breathing through a hot towel, and the mosquitos descended on her like a Thanksgiving feast. Swatting them away, she peered through the trees to the water. This part of Louisiana had a network of waterways that crisscrossed the southern part of the state through the bayous; a collection of rivers, canals, and narrow lakes that acted as a roadway. Mitra could see the near-stagnant water glinting in the sunlight on the other side of the trees.

"If the bodies were found here," she said to Haris who had come to stand next to her, "I don't think it would be because of the water. It's hardly moving."

"True," Haris said, taking a step further in. Mitra had the sudden urge to pull him back. The thought of crocodiles lurking near the bank sprung in her mind. "So, it must have been intentional. Why would someone kill all those people and leave the bodies out in the open?"

"I don't think this counts as 'in the open,'" Mitra replied. She toed at a wet log that sat near the edge of the road. "We haven't seen any cars in the last ten minutes."

"You think someone is just using this place as a dumping

ground?" Haris asked, turning to her. His hair was so bright in the sunlight, Mitra was distracted for a moment.

"Or maybe something happened to those people?" she guessed. "Weren't they all found at the same time?"

"Yeah, Larry said a local man who lives nearby saw one of them as he was driving past. He called the police, and they found the others. But they had all been missing over the last month or so. There was no connection to any of them either; they didn't know each other." Haris stood with hands on his hips, looking around.

Mitra didn't see any houses around, but there very well could be a few houseboats on the water somewhere. "Does he live close by? Maybe we should talk to him."

"Apparently, he left town right after talking with the police. Larry said he was spooked. He lives just up the road here I think," Haris said and started walking.

The two of them went a little further down the road, leaving the truck where it was. Just up ahead, between the trees, they found a hidden dirt road that led to a small house on the water. The house looked empty, and they found a boat tied to a short dock on the water. Mitra could see better here that the waterway looked like a canal maybe twenty feet wide at best, with dense trees on the other side as well.

Mitra headed straight for the front door but Haris's hand on her arm stopped her. "Hang on," he said, digging in his pocket. "Keep this on you, just in case." He pulled out a silver chain with a murky white stone on the end no bigger than her fingernail. He looped a second one around his own neck and tucked it into his shirt.

"What is it?" she asked, clasping it around her neck. The stone was roughly cut and cloudy.

"It's Reykalkan'o in Rhaptan, but most people just call it Deathstone," Haris replied. "It's basically a defiled piece of an

Anunnaki Aurastone. It emits a high-pitched ringing sound that sends most Anunnaki to their knees when they're near it —ubir included."

"I can't hear anything," Mitra said, puzzled. Only the whining of the forest and the mosquitos nipping at her ears.

Haris shook his head. "Doesn't work on humans, so it's safe for us. All Ummanu have a stash of them just in case. It's our only defense against them. Even ubir with lame abilities are stronger and faster than the average human. Not to mention they heal quicker. Keep it close if we are going to be poking around where they have been. You just have to uncover it for it to work."

Mitra nodded, gripping the stone in her hand and heading up to the door. She hadn't thought to bring any weapons as she didn't think they would encounter any ubir so easily. Mitra knocked on the door, and when no one answered, she knocked again.

Haris was peeking in a window, so Mitra tried the handle.
It was unlocked.

"Mitra..." Haris warned as she pushed the door open. It was definitely empty inside, consisting of only a few rooms that Mitra could see. A small, dirty kitchen to her left and a main living space in the middle. There was a bathroom to the right that had seen better days.

When nothing jumped out at them, Mitra and Haris started looking through the house. Something felt off. Why would the door be unlocked? There was a half-empty mug of coffee on the table, a small file cabinet toward the back that looked like it had been rifled through, and mostly empty dresser drawers.

Haris went outside for a minute before coming back. "The house runs on a generator, and it's completely turned off. I think our friend here got scared and skipped town."

"Makes sense," Mitra said, having no qualms as she looked through someone's personal belongings. "I'd be scared too if I found a bunch of bodies down the street from my house. What if he thought he would be next?"

Haris sighed and raked his fingers through his hair. "I'm going to go check out the boat."

Mitra spent a few more minutes digging through a clearly abandoned house. All personal documents had been taken and there were no personal items left. Just stray pans, lost socks, and a few buckets with a particularly fishy smell.

"Mitra!" Haris called from outside.

She went out to find Haris kneeling by the bank, inspecting the boat. "What is it?" she asked, swatting away the mosquitos again. There was an almost incessant buzzing in her ear with how many there were.

"Look at this," Haris said, pointing to the side of the boat.

What struck Mitra first was that the old motorboat was half submerged in water. The second thing she noticed was the jagged line that was burned into the side. Parts of the burn had gone all the way through, allowing water to seep in.

"Who would keep this piece of junk?" she asked.

Haris finally looked up at her, concern lacing his eyes. "I think I know why our friend left. Look here," he said, pointing to the rope that connected the boat to the short dock. "This isn't even tied on. It looks like someone threw the rope and left the boat in a hurry."

Scenarios started swirling in Mitra's mind. "Wait, wait, wait," she said, putting a hand to her head. "You think someone *attacked* the guy who lived here? And that's why he left town?" She started pacing back and forth, going through all the likely reasons.

"If I had to guess," Haris said, "I'd say the guy started

poking around and almost got caught. He hurried back before his boat capsized, ran home, grabbed what he could, and left."

Mitra turned back to face him. "What could have done that, though? A *flamethrower?*"

Haris shrugged, putting his hands in his pockets. "Probably not. It's too clean."

"Then what?" she asked.

Haris turned to her with a pointed look, and for the first time on this trip, Mitra started to feel the icy fingers of fear crawling up her back. She looked around, suddenly aware of how alone they were out here. The woods and water surrounded them, and she found her eyes darting between the shadows underneath the trees on the other bank.

"Basma's ability is agility though..." she said, quietly.

"Right," Haris said, looking out across the water with her. "Which is why I don't think Basma is behind these attacks. I think it's another ubir, maybe two. It's uncommon, but it does happen."

Mitra wiped the sweat off her forehead, unable to stop looking around. "They can do this?" she asked, gesturing to the boat. Her first experience with Anunnaki abilities was watching her best friend start glowing like a literal star. It had been beautiful and unreal and didn't frighten her. She knew Kinza and Zaid had other abilities. Kinza told her about them, but Mitra hadn't *seen* them or what they left behind. The jagged, burned line on the side of the boat would have surely gone right through flesh.

"I just don't understand why the killings weren't like other ubir kills," Haris said. "Whatever ubir is doing this must be seriously deranged. This is far more than they normally kill, and there are still five people missing." For once, Haris looked nervous, and it left Mitra with an uneasy feeling. "I'm going to call Zaid and let him know we've got a bit of a problem here," he said, turning to walk back to the house.

"I thought there wasn't reception in Rhapta?" Mitra asked.

"He'll get the voicemail when he leaves the city," Haris said and started dialing as he walked away.

Mitra gave a small smile that Haris did the same thing she did with Kinza, leaving messages for Zaid to find later. It was quickly wiped away now that she was alone with the quiet bayou around her. Rubbing away the goosebumps on her arms, she hurried to catch up to Haris.

CHAPTER 4

CUT OFF

Haris loved beef jerky. Particularly the teriyaki flavor. Especially when he hadn't eaten in hours. He and Mitra had trudged back to the truck to dig out the snacks they had buried in the glove compartment. They wanted to inspect the area a bit more before heading all the way back to town, but this was the longest he had gone without food his entire life.

"It's been three hours, you big baby," Mitra said, tapping on her phone. She was texting Larry, trying to see if they had any additional information on the five people that were still missing, or the local man who had ditched town. Haris knew that she wouldn't get much. Larry had told them everything the police department had on the case, which wasn't much. It was the reason he was asking two people with absolutely no detective experience or higher education to look into a string over murders from out of town. They were desperate.

"I have a high metabolism. Thank you very much," Haris said, tilting the bag of jerky up to dump the remaining pieces in his mouth. "Anything from Larry?"

"Not yet. He's a slow texter." She set down her phone and ate a few Cheetos from the bag on the floor before rolling it up. "How effective is the Deathstone?" she said abruptly.

"Pretty effective, but it won't stop them completely. It's still dangerous for us to be poking around here," Haris replied, grabbing the bag of Cheetos and unrolling it again. "Why?"

"How long is it realistically going to take Zaid or another venari to get here?" she asked instead.

"Depends on who is close by, but Zaid could probably get here in a day," Haris said. "Where are you going with this?"

"Well, we have very little information as is, and by the time they get here, the ubir could have moved on again. I think we should at least find out a relative area that they are in while we're waiting for the venari to get here," Mitra said.

"And how do you propose we do that?" Haris asked, licking Cheeto dust from his finger.

"Back at the house, I saw a canoe..." Mitra kept talking but Haris had stopped listening and just looked at her. From the day he met her, she had had an odd reaction to the events that had transpired with the Anunnaki and ubir. Instead of being afraid that her best friend was a different species with terrifying abilities who came home with a literal storm cloud of a man, Mitra had been *angry*. She had responded with sarcasm, voice dripping with disdain that Haris might be Anunnaki as well. He had fully expected her to scream and run away at the first sign of something supernatural. Most people thought they liked scary things like that, but the reality was when they were truly faced with it, it shattered the idea that they were safe in the world, and people got scared.

Instead, Mitra had demanded to come along when he said he would chase after Basma, and now she was suggesting they take a canoe through a swamp to find not one, but potentially three ubir hiding in the woods. He hadn't imagined the fear in her eyes when he told her what had caused the damage to the boat, but here she was, coming up with a detailed plan to go after the ubir anyway.

Did she not understand that she could *die*?

If Haris was being truthful with himself—which he tried to do frequently—he recognized the same disregard of danger in himself. He had a terrible and wonderful reflex of cracking jokes at the worst possible times.

"What?" Mitra asked with a confused look, one eyebrow raised. The sun reflected off her irises and he could see they were varying shades of brown instead of one.

"You look positively angelic today," he said with a grin, proving his own thoughts. They were both sweating through their clothes, fingers covered in cheese dust, and smelling like beef jerky.

"Pay. Attention," Mitra said, ignoring him and clapping with each word. Haris didn't want to think about what would happen if they ran into ubir though. Mitra might not be concerned for her own life, but Haris didn't want to have to bring her body back to her family. He hated funerals.

"What do you think of my idea?" she asked again.

"What was your idea again?" he asked. He had a brief thought of asking her to stay at a motel while he checked things out on his own, but then mentally laughed. The earth would freeze over before Mitra sat on the sidelines.

"I *said* there was a canoe we could use to go up the canal a bit. There's no motor so we would have to paddle, but that means it would be quieter. We could just check out the immediate area. If we don't see anything, then we head back to Abe's and tell him and Larry what we found. Do you have any weapons in here?" Without waiting for an answer, she started looking in the back seat.

"There's a machete and a hunting knife in the back, and

yes, I supposed we could take the canoe and look for monsters," he said with a sigh, digging in the Cheetos bag again. He had a bad feeling that he wasn't going to get another meal for a while.

Twenty minutes later, the two of them had found the rowboat wedged between some trees on the far side of the abandoned property. Mitra squealed when they flipped it over and a spider came scuttling out before stomping on it with her shoe.

"He could've had a family," Haris said, digging the oars out of the bushes.

"I don't care. It was gross," she said with a shudder. Haris chuckled. She was willing to hunt ubir in the forest, but a spider made her squeal?

They got the boat in the water and managed to get in with minimal splashing. Mitra had left her phone in the car, but Haris had brought his, hoping that he would get a response from Zaid. Mitra had insisted on carrying the machete, leaving Haris to tuck the hunting knife in the back of his jeans. If she felt safer that way, then he was happy.

They paddled slowly, following the natural current of the canal. There was still a bit of sunlight left in the late afternoon, but it grew dark whenever they went underneath the huge, overhanging trees. It was almost peaceful out here with the frogs croaking and the water calmly carrying them south. It wound back and forth, and the only souls Haris encountered were a few peeping eyes that poked out of the water near the banks. He didn't let himself dwell on what would happen if he fell in.

Neither Haris, nor Mitra spoke while they paddled, but Haris watched her braid swinging back and forth in front of him as her head stayed on a swivel, peering into the shadows on the banks of the canal. Haris wondered for the hundredth time why she wanted to be here.

They didn't find any more bodies or clues that screamed 'ubir this way!' There was the occasional piece of garbage but that was it. Haris was mostly focused on keeping track of where they were so they could find their way back. The waterways in the bayou could get tricky, winding back and forth, while everything looked the same.

"*Haris,*" Mitra said suddenly and with such intensity his heart stuttered for a moment. She had stopped paddling and he followed her gaze to the left bank. He didn't see anything at first, but when he saw it, he didn't know how he had missed it in the first place.

All the trees along that side of the bank had jagged lines burned into them, as if a searing line had been dragged across that part of the forest. Some of the trees had broken and fallen into the water, but most stood, half-decapitated with the same burn marks as the motorboat they had found.

Haris shoved the tip of his oar in the water, slowly the rowboat and turning it to face the bank. "Now *that* looks like a clue," he said. "I think we're on to something." He couldn't help but smile. This was good. Bad...but good because it meant they were on the right track. Something was definitely going on and it smelled of ubir business to him. As soon as Zaid called him back, he would have something worthwhile to report.

Mitra seemed less enthusiastic, whipping her head around to watch both banks in case whoever did this was close by. "I think—" she started but was interrupted by the sudden current that shoved the rowboat forward.

"Wha—" Haris looked behind them and couldn't understand what he was seeing. The canal had suddenly *risen* by nearly a foot, pushing the current downstream at a pace they couldn't paddle against.

"Haris, what's going on?!" Mitra shouted as they tried to quickly paddle back the way they came. It was useless. The water kept coming, overflowing into the forest, pushing downed trees further into the canal, and dragging muck with it. Even if they could fight against the current, they were blocked in by the debris that was closing in behind them.

"I don't know!" Haris said, trying to come up with a plan. "Paddle to shore!" It took them a moment to get onto the same page, but eventually they were working in sync to steer the rowboat to the bank. Water sloshed inside of the boat, only making them paddle faster. They hit the bank and leapt out, clawing at the mud to pull themselves away from the rushing water. It was moving way too fast for a normal canal and had widened by nearly five feet.

When they had finally pulled themselves far enough away from the water, they collapsed onto the ground.

"Was that a *flood*?" Mitra asked incredulously, waving her hands around.

"Well, it wasn't an avalanche," Haris said earning a glare from Mitra as they got to their feet. She was so easy to rile up, he couldn't help himself sometimes.

The water looked like it was still rising, albeit slower now. They pulled the canoe a little higher, throwing the oars inside. Both of them were covered in mud from head to toe and smelled of swamp water.

"What do we do now?" Mitra asked, looking at the rushing canal.

"The water should level out eventually, regardless of what caused it. In the meantime, we might as well look for more clues," Haris said, turning to look into the murky forest. It was much darker underneath the dense canopy and somehow still wet. The ground was solid, but the dirt was more like mud, sucking at his shoes.

"Ugh!" Mitra said, slinging mud off of her arms. "We are staying in a five-star hotel after this. I want a *real* shower. With*out* roaches."

"Yes, madam," Haris said sarcastically and started picking his way through the woods. Thankfully, the further in they got, the drier it was. The air never really stopped being humid, but at least they weren't walking through mud anymore. They didn't see any more of the burn marks either. Haris thought he knew where he was, but he realized they were hopelessly lost. The sudden current in the canal had pushed them down random directions and forks. They could head back to the canoe and follow the canal upstream, but he had no idea which route to go. They'd have to call someone to come and get them.

Haris stopped and pulled out his cell phone.

"I haven't seen any more of those burn marks," Mitra said, rubbing at a patch of mud on her face.

"Neither have I," Haris said. "Or anything else for that matter." His phone flickered between having a single bar and no service. There were no messages from Zaid either. He tried to call Abe's number, but it wouldn't connect.

"We also have no service, and we have no idea how to get back, even if the current has calmed down. Let's head back to the canoe and see if I have better service. It's going to get dark soon," Haris said. His stomach grumbled from his missed dinner too. The late afternoon sun danced on the treetops, but the forest floor was much darker.

They only made it a few steps when Mitra suddenly grabbed his arm. She had her head cocked and was looking deeper into the woods, the opposite way from the canoe. Haris was about to speak, but then he heard it too. He couldn't quite make out what it was. Music? Voices? Or even just a strong wind through the trees?

Without speaking, they both started walking toward the sound, being careful to stay quiet themselves. There were people who lived way out here on the waterways, and they didn't want to get caught trespassing on someone's land. There were a lot of roots and sticks to avoid so it was difficult to stay quiet. The sound was coming and going too, at one point disappearing altogether. Twice, Haris almost suggested they turn back because he could no longer hear anything, but Mitra pushed them forward.

The sound slowly got louder though, and Haris recognized it as voices, many voices. The woods were becoming much more dense here as he and Mitra slowed down, walking extra carefully. They finally came to the edge of a small lake or large river. Right in the middle was a large island where the river bisected and came back together on the other side. It was only twenty or so feet from their side to the island and Mitra and Hairs could see the other side easily.

Realizing that was where the voices were coming from, Haris stopped and pulled Mitra down, so they were hidden behind a bush.

He saw them first, the hairs on the back of his neck rising.

"Ubir..." he whispered. He had been terribly wrong in his assumption before. There weren't one or two ubir here. There were easily fifty gathered on the island. Even from here, Haris could see the crazed look most of them had and their lurching movements, almost as if they were drunk. Most were dirty and unkept, looking like they hadn't bathed in a very long time, hair wild and tangled. Some laughed hysterically at nothing at all, and others sat staring.

Mitra's eyes had gone wide as she stared at them. "They're

just...people," she said, almost confused. "Haris, these aren't—"

One of the ubir climbed to the top of a rock on the island. He was tall, *really* tall, and had long white hair that contrasted with the darkness of his skin. It was covered in muck and what might have been blood. The man jerked and lurched like the others, but his eyes were steadier—open wide as if forcing himself to see. By some unheard signal, the rest of them turned to face the white-haired man on the rock. His lips didn't move but he turned back and forth toward the group of ubir, his face increasing in intensity, eyes bulging wide. Many of the ubir cheered and raised their fists.

"What...?" Mitra whispered, looking more confused by the second.

Haris's heart was pounding. If they were caught, they'd be dead for sure. "Ubir speak telepathically like Anunnaki do," he said as quietly as he could.

The white-haired man must have still been speaking to the crowd because their energy picked up, their movements becoming almost violent. They started cheering and howling and Haris understood why when their attention suddenly turned to the right side of the island.

A group of people were tied in a makeshift cage. It was the missing humans.

Mitra gasped and Haris watched as rage quickly took over her features. "They *took* them," she said, understanding. "They're *killing* them, Haris!" she whispered furiously. She looked like she was about to launch across the river to the island and Haris instinctively grabbed her arm, holding her down.

"Shh!" he hushed her. They both watched then as the white-haired man made a sudden jerking movement with his head and twin beams shot out from his eyes like two white lasers, jerking with his head across the island, over the nearby woods, and around the ubir. Trees popped and branches exploded with the sizzling heat of the beams and Mitra and Haris ducked. The other ubir screamed in mad delight while two of the humans sobbed in their cage. The others were unconscious.

Haris grabbed Mitra again. "We have to go—"

Mitra reached for the machete she had strapped to her hip. "How *dare* they!" she said as Haris tried to pull her back. "I'm going to kill every single one of them." She made to head for the water and Haris pulled her back into the trees.

"Nope, nope, nope," he all but sang. "Time to go. We have to go *now,* Mitra." He wrapped his arms around her waist and dragged her backward as she seethed, but the commotion didn't go unnoticed.

The white-haired man's eyes snapped to Haris and Mitra across the water. The rest of the ubir quickly followed his lead, seeing the two of them scrambling back into the trees, one of them brandishing a machete. Fear, sharp and hot, spiked through Haris.

The white-haired man bellowed, and another two lasers shot across the island to strike a tree to the left of Mitra and Haris. Mitra screamed, all hope of staying hidden lost now. She stopped struggling and they turned and ran back the way they came. Haris chanced a look over his shoulder and nearly shook with fear as he saw a wave of ubir descending the island and crossing the river to the other side.

Mitra and Haris sprinted through the woods, not caring as plants and branches whipped into their faces and across their arms. Mitra's breath came in short, quick gasps and Haris wasn't doing much better. Something in the air felt different and he knew the ubir were getting closer. Thankfully none of them seemed to have the supersonic speed that Zaid did. Otherwise they would have already been caught.

Haris felt a tingling rush over his skin, and with the next step, he found his feet fumbling underneath him. Mitra gasped as the same happened to her. They both struggled as if they were newborn foals.

"The abilities!" Haris shouted at her. "Just keep going. We have to get farther away." They ran as best they could, but without the head start, they would never have made it. After a few minutes, the odd feeling on Haris's skin subsided and he and Mitra could run normally again. He could hear the shouts of the ubir getting closer though, crashing through the woods.

Just up ahead, they saw the last glimpse of sunlight reflecting off the canal where they had left the canoe. Except it was gone. The water had subsided back to its original level and there was a gentle almost imperceptible current again.

"Oh no!" Mitra exclaimed, running up to the water. They could hear the ubir behind them but couldn't see them yet. "Where'd the canoe go?!"

"No idea but we can't stop," Haris said and jumped into the canal.

"*What about crocodiles?!*" Mitra shrieked as he paddled across.

"That's not our biggest worry right now!" Haris shouted back. As if on cue, the water started to rise, and Haris felt the current quicken like it had earlier. He was about to shout at Mitra to turn back but she had already jumped in behind him. She was clearly a much better swimmer than he was, catching up to him easily with long strokes. The water rose higher and flowed faster and they swam across the canal as hard as they could. The shouting of the ubir was getting closer on the other side.

When they reached the bank, they scrambled up into the

trees, but a sizzling pop sounded right by their heads and the tree next to them had started smoking from the inside. Just up the canal, a motorboat sped toward them at full speed and standing at its head was the white-haired man. He had one foot on the prow, like he was coming for the conquest; he was eager.

The wave of ubir on the other side of the canal came into view then too. Haris spun Mitra around and they pushed their way through the trees, not looking back. Haris gasped and his lungs burned. He had *not* eaten enough today to be running like this now, or ever. They heard the commotion behind them and more shouting, like dogs on a hunt. Mitra grabbed Haris's hand and pulled them to a sharp left, and then a right, and then another left. They zig-zagged through the trees, sloshing across lowland areas where it was more mud than water, and back into the trees again. Haris thought he was going to pass out more than once, but they kept going.

Eventually the sounds of the ubir subsided and still they ran for a little while longer. Finally, Haris thought it would be better to die than run any longer so he slowed to a crawl and collapsed onto the ground, chest heaving. Mitra didn't say a word and flopped down next to him, head leaning on his shoulder. They lay there for several minutes, listening to the sounds of the forest.

"I think we lost them for now," Mitra said, still panting.

"Yeah, we should get up though. We can't stay out here," Haris said. It was getting darker by the minute and there were several ways to die out here besides the ubir. If they were lost before, they definitely weren't finding their way back now. The best hope they had would be to find someone living out here or a passing boat on one of the waterways.

Haris started patting his pants pockets frantically before groaning.

"What is it?" Mitra asked.

"My phone is gone," he said.

"Ugh. So is the machete, sorry," she replied.

"We still have the hunting knife," Haris said, pulling it out from where it was digging into his back. "And I—wait no, my Deathstone is gone," he said with a sigh.

Mitra's hand went to her throat where the chain sat beneath her shirt. "I have mine still." She started to take it off.

"No, keep it on," Haris said.

They were silent for a few moments.

"I guess we know what happened to our guy who skipped town," Mitra said.

Haris huffed a laugh. "Yeah, and why the water was rising."

Mitra turned her head. "Was that...?"

Haris nodded. "Anunnaki abilities are diverse and some of them are very powerful." He stood up and held out a hand for Mitra. "Let's get moving. We need to find shelter for the night."

Mitra let out a breath and grabbed his hand. "We're going to die out here, aren't we?"

Haris hauled her to her feet and started walking through the trees. "Probably."

THEY FOUND another waterway and followed it, careful not to stay too close to the water in case the ubir were still looking for them. It wasn't long before they found what looked like a fishing shack full of supplies just a few feet inland from the water and tree line. There was no one around and it looked like the only way to access it was by boat.

"Might as well stay here," Haris said, peering inside. Even

with the supplies, it looked mostly empty. Just a few nets, buckets, and other fishing equipment.

"Is there any water inside? I'm so thirsty," Mitra groaned.

"No," Haris said, sitting against the far wall of the small shack. "And don't drink the river water either."

"I think I might have swallowed some before," she said with a grimace. They were both beat and exhausted and could do little more than sit upright. Without saying anything else, Mitra had closed the door and sat down next to Haris. Within minutes the two of them were in a deep sleep.

Haris woke again around dawn, with Mitra still asleep against a bucket, head pillowed in her arms. He got up and went to look outside. The water was calm, and birds were singing in the foggy morning. It was much easier to see now, but that didn't make much of a difference. They were still somewhere in the Louisiana bayou with no food or water, no phone, and a horde of ubir hunting for them. It was only a matter of time before they found them again. Who knew what abilities they had?

Haris hurried back inside and, despite desperately wanting to go back to sleep, shook Mitra awake. She grumbled and wedged her head further in her arms. Haris shook her again.

"Come on, I look radiant in the morning. You don't want to miss it." He shook her again and she glared at him but at least she opened her eyes. Haris went back outside to wait for her. His legs were weak and shaky, and his lungs felt like they had gone through a cheese grater, but they needed to go somewhere else.

It took a few minutes, but Mitra finally exited the shack, glaring at the sun that was peeking through the trees now. Without speaking, they walked back into the trees and followed the waterway downstream. They walked for hours, careful not to stay out in the open, ears straining for any unnatural sounds. Mitra trudged behind Haris, and he kept looking back on intervals, making sure she was still there. The whole ride down through the country she had complained at every motel and junky gas station they stopped at, but she was quiet now. Even though he wanted to know what she was thinking, it was better that they were quiet.

Haris knew the previous evening was her first encounter with ubir, and really with Anunnaki abilities altogether. Haris had seen his fair share of venari and ubir abilities over the years and only the really outlandish ones surprised him now. Like when Kinza vanished mid-air as she fell from a rooftop. Even though Mitra knew about the abilities, it wasn't the same as really seeing them. They could be terrifying.

The abilities Haris saw the night before didn't scare him as much as how many ubir were gathered together in one place. He had never, in his entire life, ever even heard of ubir doing that. They slowly descended into madness the longer they performed the blood rite to the point where larger ambitions didn't even cross their minds. The white-haired ubir they had seen looked more lucid than the others had, but even that was a stretch.

Venari traveled alone because didn't have the numbers to travel in pairs. Most of them had difficulty taking down two ubir. How were they going to tackle *fifty*? This was bad. Really bad. Haris hoped Zaid listened to his messages as soon as possible, but the odds weren't looking good for him and Mitra.

In the afternoon, they found a small trailer home along the canal, but it looked like it had been uninhabited for years. Cobwebs stretched across surfaces covered in layers of dust. Mites crawled through the single mattress in the back and the air smelled of mold. They struck a gold mine though. There was a single gallon of unopened water in the cupboard and a very stale granola bar, but they split it and ate it anyway. After a quick rest, they were walking again.

The next two days went by with much of the same: walking in silence, looking for food, and trying not to pass out. They only found one other fishing shack like the first that had a box of oatmeal packets inside and ate them using a little of the water. It wasn't enough though. They were weak and tired, dehydrated and so, so hot. The shade of the trees provided some relief from the sun, but each breath was hot and clogged from the humidity. Haris had red bumps all over his body and so did Mitra, but they didn't see the ubir again.

On the evening of the second day, they found nothing more than a lean-to type of shack just off the bank of the water. It was hastily built from a few slats of tin. They both collapsed inside and fell into a dreamless sleep.

CHAPTER 5
THE LIST GROWS LONGER

Abe sat on his porch, watching the sunrise with his dogs at his feet. The creaking of his chair and the frogs croaking were the only sounds. He liked it that way. The noise of the city had always bothered him, especially when Pa had taken him into town when he was a boy. The world had been quieter back then though, at least from his perspective. There weren't as many ubir, and fewer venari came through. Messages between Ummanu were few and far between and he never expected a response in less than three days, let alone one.

Abe's cell phone sat on the little table next to him. Pa had crafted that table himself specifically to set his cigars on when Abe was twelve. Right now, he was more concerned with the silence coming from his phone instead of the sentimental table it sat on. It had been a day and a half since Haris and Mitra had left his house to inspect the murders at Larry's insistence. He hadn't heard from them once.

Over the years, Abe had learned to tell when something wasn't quite right. The air started to smell suspicious, and he had a hard time sleeping, even more than usual. Many times that feeling had saved him when ubir had come to town, making him stay awake at night to watch for rabid figures who tried to access his portal. The portals wouldn't work right without the Ummanu to set the right destination. That same sensation had come to him yesterday again, stronger than ever before. The dogs had howled all throughout the day, hardly eating, and Abe had paced from window to window. Anyone else might have thought he was paranoid; it had only been a day and a half since those kids left, but Abe knew better.

He had called both Haris and Mitra's phones several times with no answer. It was a bad sign. It was time for action.

Abe groaned as he leaned on his knees to stand. The largest dog hopped up and started panting. "Not time yet, Blue. Go lie down now." The dog wilted and went to lay with his brothers.

Grabbing his cell phone and punching in the numbers, Abe paced across the porch, looking out at the morning fog that was lifting as the sun crossed his yard. The line rang three times before someone answered.

"Mwha?" a voice mumbled on the other end.

"Those kids are missin'," Abe said point blank.

The voice sighed and there was some rustling. "Do you know what time it is, Abe? And that it's a Saturday?"

"Mornin' time. Those kids are missin', Larry. They ain't back yet. Somethin's wrong," Abe said.

"What do you mean missing?" Larry said, sounding more awake now. "What happened?"

"That's the thing," Abe said, pacing across the porch. "Nothin' happened. They ain't back yet. We gotta go find them. I bet they're with the others."

Larry sighed into the phone. "I'll be there in twenty," he said and hung up.

Twenty-five minutes and a mug of coffee later, Larry

appeared in a much better mood standing on Abe's porch. "You haven't gotten anything from them?" he asked.

"Nothin'," Abe said, for the millionth time. "Can you do one of those triangulation things? Find where they are?" The dogs were pacing behind Abe, sensing his distress. "Go lay down," he said to them quietly, pointing to the yard. They loped off, chasing each other.

"I've got their numbers. Let me run over to the station. I got a buddy who works in tech. We'll see if we can locate them. But Abe," Larry said, with an imploring look, "what are we gonna do if we run into those ubir? Can you fight them? Don't they have magic powers or something?"

"I've got the rifle out back, but the best I can do is try to contact Rhapta and get them to send someone. I'll wait to hear from ya though." Abe had a bad feeling. A grand total of six people dead and seven missing in the area in the last few months was astounding. What if the FBI stepped in? Things could go south real quick if they started poking around Abe's property and the portal.

"Alright, I'll call you when I've got something," Larry said and left again. It was his day off but Abe knew he was just as invested in this as he was. Who would feel safe knowing so many had already died or gone missing? Larry had a wife and kids—something Abe was never blessed with—as well as his job on the line. The stakes were high here.

Abe started on lunch as soon as Larry left, but he didn't have to wait long. His phone rang just as he was sitting down to eat.

"What do ya got?" Abe asked.

Larry was breathing heavily into the phone. "Found the last signal from Haris's phone, Abe. It's not good."

"Where are they?" Abe asked, standing.

"Last known location came from the middle of nowhere, a

few miles south of where we found the bodies, deep in the bayou. It's right in the canal, Abe. It's way out. We'd need a boat to get there."

Running a big hand over his face, Abe moaned. "Okay, can you do anything?"

"Actually, I think I can. The missing people are the highest priority at the station right now and all resources are allocated toward this case. We have two new missing persons and a last known location. We'll requisition the chopper and fly over. Try to see something."

"Can I go?" Abe asked.

"I'm afraid not, my friend. But I'll call you as soon as we get back. Should be heading out in twenty."

"Alright," Abe said, sitting back down at the table. "Just be careful, Larry. Ubir are dangerous and have all kinds of abilities. Let me know if you see anything at all."

"Will do."

Larry hung up and Abe was stuck waiting again. He ate lunch out of habit, not tasting any of it. Afterwards, he sat on the beat-up old couch in the living room and turned the tv on. He only had cable but wasn't paying attention anyway. A whimpering sound pulled him out of a reverie and he looked down to see big amber eyes looking up at him.

"I'm fine, Gats," he said. "Somethin's fishy though. And the wrong kind of fish. I can feel it." He absently scratched at the dog's head and waited for Larry to call him back. He was normally a patient man, but right now his mama would have scolded him for being so antsy if she had still been alive. By afternoon, the heat had him sweating bullets, so he grabbed a Coke out of the fridge. It only amped up his nerves.

Finally, around three o'clock in the afternoon, Larry called and Abe all but launched at the phone.

"Yea?" Abe said. "You find 'em?"

"Well…" Larry said, "I'm not sure."

"What does that mean? What did you see?"

"Me and Bobby and Phil took the chopper over the area the signal was last found in and there is a pretty narrow canal there. It also passes by Drew Collins' place just upstream a bit," Abe said.

"That the guy who left town after you interviewed him?" Abe asked.

"Yep," Larry said. "Never got much out of him and haven't been able to get ahold of him since. I'll be honest, he was a suspect at first, but things just aren't adding up. Anyways, we flew low over the area downstream, trying to see anything at all. But our gear started acting up."

"What gear?" Abe asked. "What do you mean?"

"I mean the chopper. All the dials and stats were going wonky for a few minutes and I'm pretty sure there's some sort of rave going on out in the woods."

"What?" Abe said. "A rave? Larry, what are you takin' bout? You saw people?"

"Yeah, counted nearly fifty of them. Couldn't get too close, but they were running around and acting all crazy like my daughter does when I pick her up from a concert. All willy nilly and wild. Those ridiculous clothes, wild hair. Anyway, there were a bunch of them way out there, but I didn't spot Haris or Mitra and they were pretty far from where the phone signal was."

Goosebumps had erupted across Abe's skin. The house was quiet now and he instinctively glanced toward the front door that he left open. It was bright and sunny outside but something about it felt sinister. He got up and went to his bedroom.

"Larry?" Abe asked. "Did your gear go haywire *just* before you saw those people?" He went to his nightstand and pulled out an old Ziploc bag.

"Yeah...Bobby noticed it probably right as Phil and I saw those people. Why?"

Abe tucked his phone between his ear and his shoulder so he could dump the contents of the bag into his palm. Twelve small stones tumbled out, each one roughly cut and a cloudy white.

"Those ain't people, Larry. Those are ubir."

Larry was silent on the other end of the line.

"Don't go back out there," Abe continued, the goosebumps almost painful, running across his skin. He looked over his shoulder toward the bedroom door. The hallway was empty. "Don't tell anyone to go out there. In fact, block off access to the area if ya can."

Larry was quiet. "What are you going to do?"

"I gotta make a few calls. I'll call ya back when I'm done." Abe hung up. He pulled out his cell phone, scrolling through his contacts. In all his life, he had never had to alert the entire Ummanu network across the world. Now was the time.

Suddenly the front door slammed shut. Abe whirled around as he heard a clicking sound coming down the hall toward the bedroom. His heart was slamming in his chest hard enough that he was sure he would go into cardiac arrest. Gripping the stones tighter, he moved to meet the sound.

As he turned the corner to the hall, three sets of amber eyes blinked up at him, the owner of the third whimpering.

Abe deflated, leaning against the doorjamb. "What're you boys doing in the house? Thought I told you to go outside?" He chuckled and shook his head, heading out to the living room. The wind had slammed the door shut but the dreadful sense of fear hadn't left him. There were *fifty* some ubir out there right now in his town and it was his duty to do something about it.

Abe lifted his phone again and spent the next hour dialing every Ummanu he knew to spread the word across the globe, trying to get a message to Rhapta. He would've given his left leg for that city to at least have some basic cell reception.

Let's hope this new queen is as good as everyone says.

MITRA COULDN'T OPEN her eyes. At least not during the day. Her eyelids were too heavy, being weighed down by the thick humidity that barely relented at night. They had taken to walking during the early mornings and later in the evenings. Right now, at midday, Mitra thought she would surely perish.

Something kicked her and she strained to open just a single eye. Something had kicked her.

"Are you dead?" Haris said. He lay across from her on the ground under a dense clump of trees. The last thing she expected when she had met the overly joyful and flirtatious guy in Kinza's living room was to die with him in a swamp in Louisiana. But here she was.

"Unfortunately, no," she replied. They had walked and rested for two days but had come to the conclusion they were going in circles. The day before they had found a tree with the characteristic burn marks only to find it again this morning. There were far more fishing shacks and abandoned trailer homes out here than she expected. They hadn't seen a single boat though. Why would people choose to live here? Clearly, they didn't and only used the shacks as storage or waypoints. They had scrounged up a few more bottles of water and a couple morsels of food, but not nearly enough for two fully grown adults. Especially when one of those ate enough for three.

Mitra's mind wandered a lot as they lay there and she let it drift on its own, too tired to think of a way out of here.

"Why did you want to come with?" Haris asked abruptly. He sounded half-asleep but there was never any telling with him.

"Sounded like fun," she said with a shrug he couldn't see.

"Okay now what's the real answer?" he asked. When she didn't answer right away he teased, "It's because I'm devastatingly handsome, isn't it? An air of mystery and," he took a lazy breath, "adventure…"

"Yes."

"What?" Haris quipped, lifting his head to look at her. "Really?"

"I meant yes to the last part," she said, relenting. No point in trying to retain any sense of pride when she would be dead soon. "The adventure part, and maybe a bit of the mystery."

"Oh," he said, dropping his head back down. "Explain."

She sighed. "You said that I had all the freedom in the world, but that's wrong. I have *less* freedom than you do. My parents—don't get me wrong, I love them dearly—have very high expectations of me. My entire life has been planned out by them. What grades I had to get, what friends I could have, what schools I could attend, the career I was allowed to have, and to some degree, the type of man I have to marry." She took a breath of swampy air. "I know they only want the best for me, but I want *nothing* to do with their plans." It was her turn to lift her head to look at him. "Did you know when I was ten, my parents asked me to do a full report on seven different universities so I could start preparing for college. *Ten*. And in the end, they picked for me anyway. Only a career as a doctor would be acceptable to them."

She dropped her head back down, tired from speaking so much.

"So don't do it," Haris said as if it was the simplest thing in the world.

Mitra bit out a laugh. "It doesn't work like that. If I don't, they'll be...disappointed in me. They've done too much for me to throw it all back in their faces."

It was Haris's turn to laugh. "So, you lie to them, go across the country with a guy you don't even know, chasing ubir with very scary powers, only for you to die in a swamp?"

Mitra couldn't help the tears that formed at the corners of her eyes. "Yeah," she said quietly. "I don't know why I did that." She thought about what her mother's face would look like when she found out her daughter was never coming home. It would break her.

Haris sat up enough to lean on his elbows. "I'm not trying to be mean," he said gently. "But you deserve to be happy." He looked at her for a moment. "Mitra, what do you want? I mean in life."

Her stomach twisted at the question. He had to jump right to the heart of it, didn't he? She couldn't meet his eyes as she said "I don't know" again. She wiped at the sweat trickling across her cheek.

The look on Haris's face wasn't pitying but full of enough sadness that it made her heart ache for herself. He lay back down and closed his eyes again. "I would give anything for a family like that. To have someone *waiting* for you when you got home. Someone who would notice if you died. Mitra, if I die out here, no one is going to notice. Well, I suppose the inn will notice when I don't show up for work, but that's it."

"That's not true!" Mitra shot, turning her head to glare at him. "Zaid and Kinza would notice. And *I* would notice."

Haris chuckled. "No, you wouldn't," he said. "You'd be dead with me." He laughed a little harder at that and Mitra was sure the dehydration was really setting in.

"What happened to your family?" she asked instead. "You don't have anyone at all?"

"Not really," he said. "My dad died when I was really young, so I never knew him. And my mom died of cancer about five years ago or so. Her parents aren't alive, and my dad's family isn't Ummanu, and I've never met them. It was really just me and my mom." He was quiet for a bit, but Mitra didn't say anything, hoping he would talk more. He did. "Our portal out in Sacramento had closed a long time ago. It happens sometimes. Anyway, we were told the one in Michigan didn't have anyone guarding it, so we were supposed to move out there together. She died before we got to go though, and I ended up leaving California right after her funeral. So no, I don't have anyone. It's just me."

Mitra didn't think as she struggled to sit up and crawled over to Haris and laid down next to him. "I'm sorry," she said quietly as she wedged herself next to him, shoulder-to-shoulder. "But you're wrong. You *do* have people that are here for you. Yes, Kinza and Zaid are in Rhapta but maybe we'll get to see them more than you think now that Kinza is queen. And I told you I care, so I would appreciate it if you didn't die. I'll even throw in an incentive: if we get out of here, you can borrow my parents. They'll gladly smother you in affection until you can't breathe."

Haris laughed at that, and Mitra found herself giggling too.

"Why are the Ummanu practically left defenseless against the ubir?" Mitra asked, abruptly changing the topic.

Haris's face twisted in thought. "Hmm, I don't really know. I supposed it's because we can't really fight against them."

Mitra snorted. "We may not be the first choice to hunt them down, but you could certainly be better trained. Ubir want to use the portals, right? Doesn't that make Ummanu targets?"

"You're bringing up a topic that has been discussed a thousand times over a thousand years," Haris said, squinting up at the sun. "We don't really get a choice in the matter."

"I'll ask Kinza," Mitra said matter-of-factly. "The venari numbers are low. It's silly not to at least use the Ummanu when there are so many more of you. Imagine if every Ummanu was trained, like actually trained to fight and defend themselves. More Deathstone. It would make a world of difference. Maybe not against *fifty* ubir at a time, but you could at least help."

"Yeah. Maybe they'd start giving us laqueus too," Haris said with a laugh.

"What's that?" Mitra asked, turning her head to him. His hair was damp with moisture, making it a much darker color than usual.

He waved a hand around. "It's this special rope thing that renders Anunnaki abilities useless and is painful to them but only mildly annoying to humans."

"*What?*" Mitra exclaimed. He couldn't be serious. "There's a magic rope that can bind Anunnaki and they won't *give it to you?*" She exhaled a long, annoyed breath.

"Yeah, I guess," Haris said. "To be fair, there isn't a ton of it, so usually the venari are the only ones who carry it. Maybe Kinza will find a way to make more because it would be pretty useful."

Ideas formed in Mitra's mind of all the things that could be different. The Ummanu could be better prepared for the ubir, and they could be helping the venari. Maybe it would allow better communication between Ummanu and Rhapta since it seems most Ummanu have never even met the Anunnaki leaders they are allied with. She would have a laundry list of things for Kinza to work on when she saw her again.

"So..." Haris started. "What do you think of the ubir. Crazy, right?"

Mitra remembered the tumultuous emotions that had rattled through her upon first seeing the island of ubir. The entire time she had been traveling with Haris, she had pictured the ubir as wild monsters with horns and scales and claws. Instead, they looked just like regular people. People who had gone off the deep end, but people nonetheless. She had imagined they all had families back in Rhapta who didn't know where they were or what had become of them. Had living in the city been so horrible to drive them to murder innocent people?

Seeing the people in the cage had flipped the switch for her. The ubir may not have looked like the monsters she imagined, but they were terrible through and through. They had made the decision to do this to themselves, to become *killers*. It was clear they had killed the other four people that were found and most likely every other body they had found along the trip. These ubir had chosen to become this and Mitra could never forgive them for it. Those humans were probably frightened out of their minds, not understanding what was going on.

"They're terrifying and need to be dealt with," Mitra said firmly. "No human or Ummanu deserves to die like that. Why were the ubir keeping them hostage instead of just killing them?"

Haris flung and arm over his eyes, blocking out the sun. The day was wearing by, and the sun broke through a hole in the branches. "I was wondering the same thing. Normally they kill their victims pretty quickly. They're too far gone to plan things like that. But did you see the big one with the white hair? He seemed different from the others."

Mitra shuddered. "You mean Laser Eyes? He creeped me out." That was an understatement. When Mitra had found his eyes boring into her from across the water, her insides had practically melted. She wanted to kill him and run from him in equal measure. "Maybe he's a newer ubir? They're more stable when they're...fresh, right?"

Haris choked. "Fresh? Yeah, you're probably right. I just hope Zaid got my message and hurries his butt over here. He's probably ignoring my calls and ogling at Kinza all day."

"Hey!" Mitra said, giving him a weak punch in the shoulder. "That's my friend you're talking about." She was laughing though.

"Okay," Haris said, pushing himself all the way upright. "We need to find more food, even if that means cooking an acorn."

"I haven't seen any acorns here, but we could try to fish?" Mitra replied, not getting up. She was still too tired to walk and tried not to think about the dull headache that had been slowly building all day.

"Sure, but that means you have to get up." With much struggling and Haris's help, Mitra got to her feet, feeling woozy in the process.

They fell back into their rhythm of trudging through the woods, barely lifting their feet high enough to scale the roots. They had tried to stay near the canal but it had widened and split in several directions and now looked more like a river where they followed it. The afternoon came and went with a glacial pace. They hadn't seen any further sign of the ubir and Mitra started to wonder if they were stalking them. It was that, or they had gotten so far away they would never be found. The little fishing shacks and trailer homes were almost nonexistent now too. She had half a mind to go back the way she thought they came and hunker down in one until someone showed up.

As evening started to fall, they found a boat just lying upside down off the shore. Excitement perked them up for the first time in days until they saw the huge crack running down the base of the vessel. Without a good deal of duct tape, there was no way this thing would make it more than a few feet before sinking. Haris flipped it over and she reluctantly helped him clean the bugs out before propping it against a nearby tree for some sort of makeshift shelter. Mitra knew she would sleep fitfully. The first few nights she had hardly slept a wink because of the sounds she heard all night. She could have sworn a snake had slithered by her twice in an hour.

She and Haris gathered what leaves they could find and set up sticks and branches in a sort of ring around the boat. It was practically useless but was the best they had. They were exhausted and weak and each movement felt like lifting mountains. Mitra tried not to think about what was going to happen to them, but it was becoming more and more apparent. They had joked about it at first, but even Haris stopped when they came to terms with the reality that they would never go home.

They sat, huddled together under the boat as night fell. Mitra was deliriously tired and wide awake at the same time. She had seen an alligator for the first time yesterday across the water. What if one of them ate her while she slept? The only comfort she had right now was Haris next to her. So, Mitra closed her eyes and tried to sleep, hoping that she would wake in the morning.

CHAPTER 6
OLD SCARS

Mikah trotted down the front steps of the Grand Hall, heading around the left side of the building. There had been no new updates on Eta's disturbing vision from the day prior. For now, they had to go on with their days as usual until something happened.

He had fished out a stark red tunic and pants with gold and blue detailing around the edges for the evening. One of the maids even had time to have it pressed for him so his father wouldn't have a single excuse to complain about his clothing. Dinner at his parents' home was always a critical affair. Anything was up for grabs when Raafe Sultan wanted to make sure you felt as inadequate as possible.

Mikah, a voice called from behind him as he reached the last step down. He turned and found Eta coming down the steps, hands clasped together within the folds of her sleeves. He hadn't seen her most of the day, citing that he had work to do. It was a half-hearted attempt at keeping the upcoming stress of the evening at bay.

Where are you headed? Eta said, falling into step with him as he continued around the side of the Hall. His strides were long, but she kept up effortlessly; he didn't dare be late.

To my parents, for dinner, he said.

You sound overjoyed, she said, sarcastically. *Is it going to be that bad?*

They followed the stone-tiled walkway that cut through the back gardens. Those who worked in the Hall were slowly trickling out now that the workday was over for most.

They wanted me to bring Kinza, but I thought I'd save her the misery, Mikah explained. *They'll still be upset that I'm arriving alone though.* Mikah hadn't told Eta yet about his father's little plan of controlling the queen through a marriage with Mikah... and Mikah had yet to tell his father he wasn't even going to attempt it. This was going to go well.

Well, I can go with you, if you'd like, said she, as if it was the simplest solution in the world.

Mikah looked at her from the corner of her eye. Indeed, she seemed nonplussed over his predicament. *You'll probably want to tear your hair out by the end of the night,* he said drily.

Eta shrugged. *I have nothing going on this evening.* That was that then. They followed the stone path through the expansive gardens to the large baobab-lined boulevard that bisected the northern part of the city. Just a few blocks from the Grand Hall were several residential plazas for some of the wealthiest families in the city. Homes here were so large, only three to four resided in each plaza, and each home had enough rooms to realistically house several families. It was in one of these plazas that Mikah turned into, passing the large statue of an ancient warrior in the fountain in the center. The last home had a multitude of windows with wide shutters to block out the afternoon sunlight. The flat-topped roof was covered in an extensive variety of greenery, with vines spilling over the side of the house.

Mikah knocked on the double wooden doors and waited with Eta at his side. Today he had to pull down a different mask than the one he usually wore. This one felt more like armor to him, and he had to mentally warn himself not to take his father's remarks to heart.

The door opened and they were met by the stoic face of a servant. *Good evening,* she said to Mikah and looking Eta over. She probably realized this was *not* the queen he was supposed to bring. She gave a small but polite smile anyway. *Your parents are in the courtyard. I will lead you there.* She turned and went deeper into the house, leaving Mikah and Eta to follow behind.

The house was rectangular with a large courtyard in the center, filled with a few fruit trees and chairs to hide in the shade. The blue tiles that covered the ground each had a detailed character painted from different points in Rhaptan history. It was an excess that had cost a fortune, but the Sultans had money to spare.

The servant—Mikah could never remember their names— led them through another set of open double doors. His parents, who were seated beneath the mango tree, looked up expectantly. *Mikah Sultan has arrived with his...guest,* she said and gave a short bow before stepping to the side.

Eta, these are my parents Raafe and Sholeh Sultan, Mikah said gesturing to his parents. Eta gave a serene bow of her head. *Mother, Father, this is Eta Nahdi, an Advisor to the queen and Seer of Rhapta.*

Mikah discovered there were a few other servants nearby when they gasped at Eta's name. It wasn't often that old Hakim's Apprentice entered the home of civilians. Mikah knew that Eta spent most of her life inside the Grand Hall and spent little of it out in the streets. Hakim had been revered by most in the city and many knew of his Apprentice but never saw her.

Raafe was not one of those to be impressed. In fact, his

mouth had fallen into a frown under the hollows of his cheeks. He had the ankle of one long leg resting on the knee of the other and leaned back in his chair as if he were king, not bothering to rise to greet his guest.

I thought the queen was coming, Raafe said, looking Eta over with clear disapproval.

The queen was occupied, Mikah said. He wasn't wrong. Just half an hour ago, Kinza had ended their daily Advisors' briefing citing that she and Zaid had a *special* meeting that couldn't wait. Mikah would have believed her had it not been for the waggle of her eyebrows.

Raafe's frown did not let up and a tense silence permeated the courtyard. Sholeh's voice broke softly through the silence. *Shall we sit down to eat?* She was a thin woman, always with an elaborate hairstyle and braids that looked like they were too tight. She never complained once though. Mikah knew she did it to please his father; Sholeh would never speak out against her husband.

Raafe nodded and he and Sholeh follow the servants inside. Mikah and Eta exchanged a look. He tried to warn her.

The four of them trailed back into the house, down the hall to the dining room. It was a cozy space with the traditional low tables of Rhapta and wide, beaded cushions to sit on. As a child, Mikah had always found the elaborate cushions too uncomfortable as the beads dug into his backside. They sat down around the table and soon the servants brought out several trays of steamed rice, spiced vegetables, and bowls of fried mangoes in a sweet cream sauce. Pots of a bitter tea were set down as well amid the dishes.

Without preamble, Raafe dug right into the food. Mikah didn't dare grumble over the fact he hadn't said one word to their guest, but Eta looked like she was handling her own. The food was delicious but was quickly ruined when Raafe started speaking.

Mikah, what progress have you made in regard to our last conversation? he asked around a mouthful of vegetables.

He's asking about this now? Mikah thought to himself.

Eta glanced at Mikah before he spoke. *As of yesterday, we've approved the building of four new schools to accommodate the children that have come in from the outskirts,* Mikah said nonchalantly.

Raafe waved a hand in his direction. *No, no. The other conversation we had a few days ago. About your future.*

If Mikah hadn't known his father so well, he would have been baffled at the blatant disrespect he was showing to Eta by plotting to manipulate the queen right in front of her. But Mikah had played this game with his father a thousand times, and he wouldn't make it easy for him.

Oh! Right, Mikah said with a snap of his fingers. *I was able to get the cistern repairs approved today and the work starts next week. I know how you have an issue with clogged pipes in the house.*

Raafe's face fell into a deeper annoyance, and he shook his head to himself before sending the spear right back. *Well, there is still time left in the day for you to do something productive, I suppose. Maybe you should stop flirting with every woman that catches your eye. You would have more time to accomplish something worthwhile.*

His words were laced with a touch of acid. Even though Mikah and his father were the only ones speaking, the room had gotten a touch quieter. When Mikah didn't respond, Raafe continued. *For example,* he said, pointing at Mikah as he chewed, *when are the Elders going to be holding court again? It's been weeks!*

Eta, who had been quietly eating her food this entire time, spoke up before Mikah had a chance to throw a barb back at his father. *Excuse me,* she said, voice sounding like crystal. *I don't mean to interrupt, but the Elders will no longer be holding court since they no longer control the city. The Elders that chose to retain their positions will continue working as representatives of their respective areas, but the Queen will start holding weekly court sessions that will be open to the public in two weeks. Her formal Advisors will be in attendance as well.*

Raafe was looking at her like he forgot she was there, but didn't respond, going back to his food. Eta's face was etched in confusion at his response. She didn't know how deep Raafe's dislike of the queen went but Mikah was sure she was catching on quick.

The sounds of eating filled the room for a few minutes before Mikah asked pleasantly, *Mother, how have you been? I didn't see you when I was here last.* It was true, but that wasn't unusual. Sholeh frequently complained of headaches that required her to lie down but refused to see one of the healers.

As usual, Raafe interjected before his wife could speak. Mikah was getting really tired of the way this evening was going. *Your mother hasn't been feeling well as of late. If you wouldn't give her so much to worry about, maybe she would be feeling better.*

What's there to worry about? Mikah asked a bit sharper than he intended. Mentally, his mask was slipping.

Well, Raafe said slowly, as if to a child, *she's worried about the queen and the lack of direction she has. The queen needs a strong, stable hand to guide her. You are more than capable to do so, but you spend your time dallying around the city, doing what? Helping degenerates?*

Eta's mouth popped open and Mikah wondered if he'd lost all credibility with her. How could she stand to be friends with someone who was clearly raised by this man? He would be surprised if she never spoke to him again from the embarrassment of the evening alone.

Mikah reigned in his rising temper, but he had had enough. *You may not have been paying much attention to what is happening in the city, Father, but the queen is doing quite well so far. Yes, everything is a little unstable at the moment due to the changes in government, but give her time.* Before he changed his mind, he added, *Maybe we should let the queen do this on her own. Without the heavy-handed guidance you speak of.*

He had made his position on the matter known and there was a slight relief in tension from his shoulders. He had all but outright told his father he wouldn't be going along with his plan. The room had gone silent again; even his mother had stopped eating and only stared at her plate. Raafe's face had gone stony with barely controlled anger, fists balled on the table.

Mikah, I will speak to you in my office, he said and stood.

As he walked out, Mikah looked to his mother one more time, hoping she would say something, but she kept her eyes downcast. With a sigh he said, *I'll be right back,* to Eta and followed his father to receive whatever punishment he saw fit.

ETA WATCHED Mikah leave the room, at a loss for words. He had said his relationship with his father was strained, but she hadn't thought it was this bad. She sat there, with half of her food uneaten and one of her hosts across from her who had yet to speak to her.

Since she had entered the house, the usual images that flashed in her mind had turned to cracked tiles and dead grass. It was a dead feeling and she longed for the night to be over. It was clear that Raafe had ill intentions towards the queen. Had Mikah known about this? No wonder he was the way he was with a father like that. She didn't know how she would have handled growing up like that. Yes, she had been an orphan and that has its own struggles, but she always had Hakim and he never once raised his voice at her.

Mikah and his father must not have gone far because Eta could hear them down the hall from another room. It was quiet at first, but the mental voices started to get louder. Eta and Sholeh made no attempt to pretend at eating and the servants in the room made no move either. They were all listening to Raafe berate his son.

"—and I have never heard such disrespect—!"

"You never asked—"

"—do as you're told, or I—!"

There were incoherent mumbles and then, *"You are a disgrace and will never be the man Tahir was!"*

"I never wanted to be! Why can't you—"

"—pathetic excuse of a—"

Rage rose quickly under Eta's skin. For a half second, she debated keeping her emotions in check, but Raafe's voice was getting louder and Mikah's was getting quieter. It twisted her stomach and she found herself standing and marching toward the door.

Sholeh finally found her voice. *Advisor, don't—* but Eta was already storming down the hall with one of the servants running behind her.

Raafe's office was indeed just down the hall to the right, the door had been left open a crack and Eta shoved her way inside. Raafe had paused mid-sentence to gape at her audacity, but Eta didn't care. She strode right up to him and said, *You're wrong!*

What— Raafe started but Eta didn't give him the chance.

I said you're wrong, she repeated. Anger simmered and she couldn't hold it back. *Every single one of those things you said to Mikah were wrong. I cannot fathom how a parent couldn't be proud that their son saved the queen's life or became one of her most trusted Advisors. I cannot even comprehend that you could call the man who spends every waking hour working to make Rhapta a better place pathetic. You, Raafe, are the pathetic one and you could never be half the man he is!*

Raafe was still gaping at her like a fish out of water. Mikah stood frozen next to her, and she finally got a grip on that burning anger, pushing it down enough to take a deep breath. She looked at Raafe again and hoped he saw the contempt in her eyes. *Dinner was lovely,* she said, calmer this time, *but the company was deplorable. Your future is murky, Raafe. I would tread carefully.*

With that she turned, grabbed Mikah by the arm, and didn't stop until they had gone back through the house and out the front doors into the plaza. There, she let go of Mikah and huffed a breath as embarrassment started to settle in.

Did she really just do that? Did she just throw insults at one of the richest men in the city? And Mikah's father at that? Hakim had always taught Eta to control her emotions lest her visions control her. She had always been adept at doing so, but something about the way Mikah slowly stopped fighting back had hit her like a brick. No one deserved to be treated like that.

The sun was on its last legs and shadows were long as Eta started walking across the empty plaza. Heat burned her cheeks, and she couldn't bear to look Mikah in the eye yet, even though she heard his footsteps behind her. She barely made it across the plaza but the urge to at least apologize overcame her and she turned to face him.

His face was oddly blank, and she worried that she had actually gone too far in yelling at his father. She inhaled to speak but Mikah stepped forward and wrapped his arms around her. Eta was shocked for a moment, but finally looped her arms around his waist as well. Maybe he wasn't as mad as she expected him to be, and she found the feeling of being pressed into his chest comforting. So, she let herself stay there for a moment, closing her eyes and she felt him rest his chin on the top of her head. They stood that way for a long time before Mikah spoke.

Is my father's future really murky? he asked. That wasn't what she expected him to say.

No, Eta replied, *but he doesn't need to know that.*

She felt the rumbling in his chest as his shoulders shook with laughter. *Thank you,* he said, holding her tighter. Eta didn't object and didn't care if anyone was walking by and saw two of the queen's Advisors embracing in the street.

All of the stress of the evening started to melt away and she could feel Mikah relaxing as well now that they were out of that house. It was almost silly to have gotten so worked up over the words of a man who had little power over the city when there were so many other things going on.

Ever since Mikah had helped her during the massive vision she had down in the quarries, their relationship had become something else. More than friends, but she wondered if he felt the same. She didn't know where their relationship stood, but for the moment she was perfectly content to stay in his arms.

After a while, Mikah pulled away to peer at her face. *Come on. I hardly ate dinner and I know a great fried plantain seller that's open late.* There was a faint smile on his face, and she knew he wasn't mad at her at all.

Eta nodded. *That sounds great.* Maybe they would talk about what happened between them later, but for now Eta would let things be.

IN HIS ENTIRE LIFE, Zaid never thought he would find bliss in the darkness of a coat closet. He also didn't imagine he would be sharing the space with the queen of Rhapta. Yet, here they were, trying to stay as quiet as possible so no one would find them. That was hard when the queen kept giggling.

Kinza, if you don't stop laughing, we're going to get caught, he mumbled into her annoyingly soft neck.

That only started another fit of laughter from her and he quickly covered her mouth with his to muffle the sound. *I'm the queen!* she mumbled in his head. *Who's going to catch me?*

There was an ever-lengthening list of people would disapprove if they were caught. Zaid had found that all good things came with a price. Kinza was finally his after so long of pretending to himself that he could never have her, but with her becoming queen, it was becoming increasingly difficult to find time to spend with her that didn't involve government meetings and public audiences. He knew that she had fully committed herself to taking care of the Anunnaki, but it was an odd feeling to be jealous of an entire city.

So, taking the time they had before it got whisked away, Zaid kissed her again in answer. The movement caused her to step back, and right into a bucket, which then caused a broom to clatter to the ground.

They both froze waiting to see if someone heard. When nothing came, he felt her fists tighten in his shirt to pull him closer. The grin had barely spread across his lips when an insistent knocking came at the door.

Your highness! came a voice on the other side of the door.

Maybe if we're quiet, he'll go away, Kinza said in Zaid's mind.

He did not, in fact, go away. The knocking even became more insistent. *Your highness, there's an emergency!*

Zaid exhaled in annoyance. *Should I schedule some time with you next quarter?* he grumbled to her before disentangling their limbs so he could open the door. Zaid pushed it open and found a young messenger in a brown shirt and pants standing outside the door, looking as confused as Zaid felt—minus the annoyance.

What is it? Zaid asked, slightly more of a growl that he would have liked.

I'm glad you're...here, sir, the young man said. *You both need to get to the house of the venari, quickly.*

Zaid exchanged a look with Kinza who had finished readjusting her hair. *What's going on?* she asked, all business now.

Two venari showed up with a message for both of you, the messenger said. *They won't say what happened until you arrive.*

TEN MINUTES LATER, Zaid and Kinza were trotting up the front steps to the place Zaid called home for so many years. He didn't knock and just pushed the doors open. Savar was standing in the center of the training ring with two venari Zaid hadn't seen in a long time. Two older men who hadn't quite reached their years of retirement yet. Their faces looked grim.

Well? Kinza said, not wasting time. *What happened?* They stopped in the middle of the ring with the others.

Savar had his arms crossed and looked affronted at the fact he wasn't allowed to wring the answers from his own venari before the queen arrived. *Yes, let's get on with it.*

The first venari spoke up. *Sorry, we thought it was best this came to the queen and Zaid Hatem, considering it's regarding their friend.*

Zaid felt Kinza stiffen beside him and he grabbed her hand, not caring who saw. *Haris?*

The second man nodded. *We were both contacted separately through the Ummanu, as many other venari are probably being contacted right now a well. There is a message traveling through the Ummanu network, a message that was to be delivered to you immediately. It seems the Ummanu Haris Williams went* looking *for an ubir a few days ago in the southern United States but went missing.*

The other venari shook his head at that, as if baffled that a human would go after one of the ubir.

The second man continued. *The Ummanu in that area was able to use local forces to discover that a pack of ubir were living in the area Haris went missing.* The man looked like he was going to be sick.

How many? Savar asked, but it looked like he understood already.

When the man didn't immediately answer, panic started to flood Zaid's own veins. *How many?!* he barked.

Nearly fi-fifty, the man stuttered, eyes wide.

By the Creator, Savar swore, putting his hands on his knees.

Was he alone? Kinza asked the man. She gripped Zaid's hand so tight there was a chance he would bruise.

Who? the first venari asked, looking confused.

Haris, Kinza said, *Was Haris alone when he went missing?*

Oh, actually no, I think someone was with him, he replied. *Another human.*

Kinza gasped, *Mitra.* Zaid started to feel heat coming from her and he hoped she wasn't about to burst into flames; it just wasn't the time.

Breathe, Kinza, he said, only to her. *It's going to be fine. They're fine.* Although he wasn't actually sure of that. Haris had been his friend for years now, one of his best friends if he was being honest. Zaid was the one who tasked him with keeping an eye on Basma, and he would hate himself forever if Haris—and Mitra—died because of it.

Savar had recovered and Zaid felt an old twinge of fear as he started bellowing orders, calling down the other venari that were up in their rooms. Zaid watched as Savar gave the order for every venari in-house to head immediately to the United States. He asked the first two men for the exact location and demanded Zaid give them Haris's number so they could try to contact him when they left the city. The call went out and soon every venari within the western hemisphere was mandated to drop all current assignments to head to Louisiana. Fifty ubir could easily destroy an entire city within a few hours, depending on the abilities they had. If they did so, causing humans to rediscover the Anunnaki too soon, they could quickly have the army Tahir had brought right back on their doorstep. It would be catastrophic if humans found out too soon, and like this.

The house of the venari was soon a flurry of movement and ordered chaos. It was rare that there was so much happening at once within the small confines of the building, and it made Zaid feel uneasy. Old training kicked in and he moved toward the stairs to the second floor.

Where are you going? Kinza blurted out. She looked like she was struggling to contain the flames that would easily ignite from her skin. They were smothered for the moment though.

To gather supplies and weapons. I'll need to leave immediately, he said.

You're going? Kinza asked, brows knitted. He desperately wished they were back in the storage closet so he could ease the worry from her face.

Zaid looked over to Savar who had heard her question. He gave a quick, firm nod. *We're both going,* Zaid said to Kinza. When was the last time Savar had left the city? It had been years and he seemed to remember that as he pushed past Zaid to head to his office where the ink was. They would all need to touch up their tattoos immediately.

Then I will too, Kinza replied, moving to follow him.

Zaid shook his head. *You're the queen now, Kinza. If you abruptly leave, the city will panic. They need you here.* At the frustrated look on her face, he added, *I'll find them both. Mitra will be fine.*

Silver rimmed her eyes at her friend's name, but she gave a reluctant nod. *Okay, let me know if you need anything. I'll go alert the Advisors so they're aware.* She turned on her heel and strode out of the building, head held high.

Zaid would do everything he could to find their friends, but doubt crept in his mind. *Haris, what have you gotten yourself into?* He climbed the stairs to join Savar.

CHAPTER 7
INTO THE HORDE

Night had fallen some time ago, but Mitra had difficulty remembering when. She and Haris had walked on for a little while longer only to discover they had walked in a circle...again. They came across one of the small storage shacks at the edge of the canal and had practically fallen inside. She couldn't remember how long ago that was. She had been in and out of it since then. Her eyes would close and when she opened them, she would have no idea how much time had passed. Had they been here days? Weeks? Months? It couldn't have been that long because you couldn't survive more than a few days without water. At least humans couldn't.

They hadn't seen any of the ubir again either, but they did stumble across some of the burn marks on the trees they saw before. It wasn't a great sign, only meaning that they had walked in circles without getting anywhere.

She was huddled in the corner of the shack now, Haris across from her. Closing her eyes again, she realized he had been talking to her when he nudged her with his foot.

"Hey, you alive?" he asked, looking like he was about to meet death himself. His hair had darkened from sweat and dirt and dark circles hung under his eyes. She could have sworn he had lost weight as well, but she was probably imagining things. It would only have been a few days.

"Mmalive," she mumbled.

"I'll go look for food again in a bit," Haris said, trying to cheer her up. "I think I saw some leaves that I'm sixty percent sure that we can eat."

"Whabout the otter forey?" she barely managed to get out. In truth, she no longer felt hungry or thirsty; she only wanted sleep.

"Eh, I'm willing to risk it," Haris said. "Now would be the time." He kept talking but Mitra dozed off again. She woke when he shuffled to his feet, saying that he was going to look for food. She hummed a response but quickly fell asleep again.

Just like the last few times she slept, she had no idea how long it had been when she opened her eyes again. It was still dark, and she could just barely make out that Haris wasn't back yet. It could have only been five minutes, or it could have been hours. Mitra rested her head on her knees and tried to fall asleep again, but a minute later she heard Haris's footsteps coming back, walking softly through the shrubs.

She closed her eyes again, waiting for him to come in and tell her he couldn't find anything, but he never did. He stopped just outside the door without coming in. After a few seconds, something deep in Mitra's mind started ringing bells. Opening her eyes, she could make out the outline of the door. She was about to call to him when the handle turned, and the door opened inward slowly.

A tall figure—too tall to be Haris—was silhouetted in the moonlight. She couldn't make out the face, but the long white hair was unmistakable. Mitra's heart gripped like a vise in her chest and her muscles froze in place. If she had had anything in her bladder, it would have soaked her pants.

"No..." she moaned as the figure stalked forward, raising a fist, and Mitra soon found herself sinking into blackness.

HARIS STUFFED another handful of wet leaves in his pocket. It must have rained the night before because everything was covered in a layer of dampness. They had stayed in the tiny shack all day, too tired to move. When Mitra had started responding less and less, a surge of adrenaline slugged its way through his veins, urging him to get up and try to find something to eat, just one more time.

Wandering around the dark was probably not the smartest thing he had ever done. But neither was going hunting for creatures with powerful abilities that could literally heal faster and didn't need food and water frequently. At least he was consistent with his dumb ideas.

He had been out here for almost thirty minutes, pockets bursting with leaves, vines and a suspicious looking item that looked a bit like a large, green acorn. It didn't matter if they were poisonous as they would be dead soon at this rate. He decided to try one of the leaves first and shoved one into his mouth. Despite the wetness, it was bitter and thick, and he had a hard time swallowing. Now to wait.

Haris picked his way through the roots and vines that covered the ground, keeping his eye on the moonlight that reflected off the canal. Did crocodiles sleep in the water, or did they come up on land? He walked slower to see where he was going.

The shack came into view, and he wondered how they were

going to choke down the leaves without any water. As he got closer, he noticed the door to the shack was open.

"Mitra?" he whispered, concern causing him to walk faster.

"Mitra...?" he asked again as he pushed the door open.

Empty. The shack was empty.

Haris stepped back outside and looked around, trying to peer through the darkness. "Mitra?" he asked again, a little louder. Maybe she had gone to relieve herself, but something in his stomach was making him think otherwise. It was that or the leaf.

He circled the shed, calling her name softly into the gloom, but only the croaking of the frogs and cicadas responded. Haris didn't think his heart could beat as fast as it was right now.

"No, no, no, no!" Haris said, pacing back and forth, calling her name again. She was gone. Mitra was gone.

That was when Haris noticed the canal. Out here in the bayou, it hardly ever moved, barely a current. Under the moonlight, he could see the barely perceptible waves up the canal that lapped against the bank on either side. They were moving away and dissipating with each second.

"*No...*" Haris said, gripping his hair. The ubir had found them.

MITRA WOKE to the worst headache she had ever experienced. Her entire skull felt like it was throbbing hard enough to pop her eyeballs and the light that tried to make its way through her eyelids was a personal attack. The groan that escaped her was involuntary.

Where was she? What happened? Before she could answer those questions, something was pushed to her lips and a coolness spilled over her jaw, down to her shirt. It was enough to get her to peel her eyes open. Despite the light that was lancing in through the window, she could see she was in a dark room. Her eyes were blurry at best, and shapes moved in the shadows. The pounding in her head was so painful, she didn't even care if they were there to kill her.

Again, something was pushed to her lips, and she realized it was a small bowl filled with water. Instincts took over and she had gulped the entire thing down in seconds. "More," she croaked. Her throat was raw and she felt nauseous.

The bowl was brought back to her lips and again she drank the entire thing. "More," she croaked again, waking up a bit more.

"There won't be enough for the rest of us," a timid voice said. Mitra finally was able to make out the face of a woman kneeling next to her. She had short brown hair and hazel eyes and looked miserable.

Confused, Mitra slowly struggled to sit up, her head spinning enough that she was sure she would vomit the water she had just drank. Looking around, she saw four more people huddled in the small room they were in. Mitra felt a swaying again and covered her mouth. "I think I'm going to throw up," she said.

"Don't you dare waste that water," a man's voice growled at her. A blond man with a pockmarked face glared at her from the corner.

The first woman pursed her lips in her direction and placed a soothing hand on Mitra's shoulder; she must have been a mother. "We're in a houseboat," she explained. "It's the swaying of the water that you feel. Here, eat this. It'll help." Her voice was sweet, with a faint southern accent. She handed Mitra a handful of cut up banana. The smell alone would have sent her to her knees had she not already been sitting. It was gone in three bites and the hunger pains she hadn't felt before became more insistent.

"What's your name, honey?" the woman asked.

"Mitra." She finished her food. "Do you have any more?" she asked.

"No!" the blond man snapped. "Sarah, we didn't get any additional food to split with her. What we have is for us."

"What does it matter? We're not going to be alive much longer," whimpered a young woman, barely older than Mitra, sitting against the wall. All life was vacant from her eyes, but Mitra could see the tracks the tears had traced through her dirty face. There was another older woman asleep in the corner and a man rocking and muttering next to her. He didn't look like he was aware of what was going on, or if he did, it had driven him to madness.

Memories from the night before slammed into Mitra's already pounding skull. The white-haired ubir had come to take her. Where was Haris then? Had he been taken too, or did he get away?

"Here, you can have mine," the woman, Sarah, said, handing her two slices of plain bread.

Mitra took them greedily, wobbling between hunger and nauseousness. "Are there others?" she asked around a mouthful of bread. She wished they would give her more water.

The blond man shrugged. "None that are alive, unless they are being kept somewhere else."

"Where are we exactly?" Mitra said, seeing only trees out the window.

"We're docked on some island in the bayou, but we have no idea where," Sarah said, easing back against the wall.

As Mitra ate, the pains in her stomach subsided a little and the nauseousness eased. "How long have you been here?"

"That man has been here for a at least a few weeks," Sarah said, nodding toward the man rocking back and forth. "Since then, we've all arrived at various times. There were others but..."

"They were killed," Mitra said, understanding.

Sarah nodded. "Does anyone know you're here? Where were you taken from?"

Mitra nodded. "There are a couple people that know I'm in Louisiana and I was with a friend when I was caught. At least he was supposed to be there but I'm not sure what happened. We had gotten lost in the woods." She didn't think it was a great idea to mention that she and Haris had been *looking* for the ubir. That would open a can of worms she wasn't ready to deal with.

"I'm so sorry," Sarah said.

"Why?" Mitra asked.

"Because your friend is probably dead already," the blond man said dully.

"Quiet, Nick!" Sarah hissed at him. "You don't need to be mean to the poor girl. She's probably in shock."

The man, Nick, snorted. "It's true. We're all going to be dead soon. Those people can *do* things," he said, pointing out the window. "I bet it was the government trying to hide their botched experiments. Just dump 'em out here, not like anyone would notice," he scoffed. The young woman in the corner whimpered again.

"Don't listen to him," Sarah said, touching Mitra's arm. "But he isn't wrong. I don't know what they are but they're not human." She shuddered.

Mitra didn't want to confirm how right she was, so she asked, "Why are they keeping us in here instead of just killing us right away?"

"We're part of a sacrifice," Nick spit out. "But their leader likes to...play with us before they kill us. They use their magic to drive us mad before slitting our necks and wrists and tossing us in the river."

Despite the heat, Mitra shivered. This was exactly what she had been afraid of. How could she have been so stupid? She was the one who urged Haris to go looking for the ubir, and now he could very well be dead. She didn't dare think about that too long, focusing instead on the hot anger that she had buried down deep since she had first seen the ubir.

Getting up slowly, she went over to the little window and peered out. She could see that they were on the river but docked near the island on the other side of the boat. The other side of the room had a door, and she didn't need to try the handle to know it was locked. The five other people in the room stayed in their corners, looking like they had already accepted their fate.

One way or another, Mitra was going to get out and get home to her family. No way was she going to allow those monsters to take her away from her family, even if she was the one who got herself into this.

It must have been close to the afternoon when they heard footsteps slam onto the deck above them. Sarah had told Mitra that the room they were in was below deck of a small house-boat. The ubir came every morning with barely enough food and water to last them the day, and then twice more to take them to relieve themselves. Mitra thought it was odd that they would do all that to keep them alive when they were just going to kill them. But then again, what fun is a dead mouse to a cat?

The young woman, whose name Mitra discovered was

Rachel, started sobbing the moment the sound came from above. Nick swore and the others huddled away from the door, other than the madman who just kept on rocking and muttering to himself.

The sound of heavy feet coming down the stairs had Mitra's heart quickening, but she didn't cry. The little bit of food and water had given her a mountain of strength, at least mentally if not physically.

The door was snatched open, and the first thing Mitra noticed was the heavy, labored breathing of the man that came in. It was less like he was out of breath, and more like a dog when it got excited. A short, well-muscled man with a sloppy haircut pushed his way inside, a slight grin on his face. His eyes were wide and one of them was bloodshot, but he focused on each of them individually, belying a sanity Mitra doubted he had.

"Let's go, all of you," he grunted in a thick accent. Mitra thought it sounded vaguely like Zaid's had, but more garbled.

They all exchanged glances but got up and followed the man out in single file. Once they got up on deck, the sunlight pierced Mitra's eyes and the headache came throbbing back. She could see the island to her left filled with trees but she thought she could barely make out the other side. The man led them off the boat down to the trees by the shoreline where they could do their business.

As they walked into the trees and shrubs, Sarah caught Mitra eyeing the other bank across the river. "Don't even think about it," she whispered. "That one," she said, pointing to the man they came to get them, "I don't know how, but one woman tried to run away and her feet sunk into the ground almost to her knees. They killed her that day. We can't run away."

"We'll see about that," Mitra said and found the man staring at her as if he knew what she was thinking.

On the way back to the boat, she caught a glimpse of the other ubir on the other side of the island. They were getting loud again and many of them called and hollered in their direction, laughing the whole time. Mitra also swore the man that was leading them was staring holes into her back.

Once they were below deck again, the man slammed the door shut and locked it, and they were alone with only the single window for light. Mitra found a place by the wall and sat down with the others.

IT WAS evening when they came again. Mitra's stomach was already cramping with hunger and her headache was in full force again. Somehow it felt worse than it had the last few days.

This time it was a woman that came in. She was tall, really tall, and had a huge bloody scar on her right arm. It took Mitra a few moments to realize it was the Anunnaki tattoo, but it had become warped and all the lines were a jagged red, as if it was infected.

The woman seemed slightly saner than the man. She scowled at the six humans and something about the look on the others' faces made Mitra understand that this was not a normal visit. The young woman, Rachel, was hyperventilating and Nick had his faced turned as far away as possible from the woman. But neither of them was her target. Instead, she reached with long fingers for the madman who continued to rock back and forth, hauling him to his feet. Sarah started crying then and Mitra knew what was going to happen.

The woman hauled the man out into the hall and slammed the door shut. They heard the click of the lock. The sun had started to set but the noise from the ubir had continuously gotten louder throughout the day. As soon as the door closed, Mitra rushed to the window, but it faced away from the island.

It only took a minute or two and a cheer rose from the ubir. Mitra's cellmates started shaking and she wanted to cover her ears but she had to find a way out and that meant listening for every possible piece of information. She sat by the open window and listened to the sounds that came from the island.

She never heard any talking, but she figured it was because all Anunnaki spoke telepathically. She only heard the ubir's cries in delight. Suddenly she heard something that crackled and zapped, followed by a lonely shout. Was that lightning? Electricity?

Soon the sounds of a fight broke out and she wondered if the ubir fought amongst themselves normally. They were hardly sane and all longed for bloodshed according to Haris. Maybe she could use that to her advantage.

As the sounds of the madman's torture continued, Mitra could no longer hold back her thoughts of Haris. What if he really was dead? He hadn't been there when she woke but they could have easily found him in the woods while he was out looking for food. If she survived this and he was dead, she knew she would never forgive herself for dragging him out here. How could she face Kinza and Zaid again either?

She hung on to a tiny shred of hope that the ubir hadn't found him. He was still in dire need of food and water, but if she could just get out and get to him, they could try to find their way out of the bayou.

The manic sounds on the island went on for nearly an hour before it started to get quiet. Whatever they were doing wasn't loud enough to reach the boat, but then a cry of delight went up, louder than before, and Mitra knew the madman was dead.

Sarah cried softly and the older woman, who had been silent the entire time, started to pray.

"What happens now?" Mitra asked quietly.

Sarah wiped at her eyes. "Nothing. Tomorrow we do it all over again."

It was the first night in days that Mitra couldn't sleep, so she huddled with the others by the window and spent the hours plotting her escape.

CHAPTER 8

SHADOWS IN THE FOREST

Haris crouched in a spot of sunlight, hoping his clothes would dry faster so they would stop chaffing. He couldn't afford to stand, in case he was spotted, but he took the moment to eat another of a weird fruit he had found.

After Mitra had been taken, he had immediately jumped into the dumbest plan he had had in the last week. And that was saying something. He knew there was only the slimmest of chances that he would find Mitra and the ubir on his own, so he did the only thing he could; he followed the trail.

The canal had had the barest remnants of a wake from the boat the ubir had used and Haris followed it at a full sprint. Or as close to one as he could manage in the dark, through the woods, and malnourished.

He tried to make as little noise as possible, hoping to avoid the notice of the ubir. They had traveled slowly so as not to spook their prey, but that made it easier for Haris to follow. It was still difficult though, trying to keep up with a boat. The canal wound back and forth and split a few times, and at one point Haris had needed to cross. It was a split-second decision to jump into the canal in the middle of the night—yet another of his dumb ideas. But if he didn't hurry, Mitra would be lost, so he swam across a narrow section and waded out the other side. His waterlogged clothes made it hard for him to run after that, and the boat was getting further away with each minute.

Haris lost it after a few minutes though and spent a few more minutes panicking again before he noticed the noise he heard in the dark. He recognized it instantly as the ubir on the island, rowdy and chaotic in the middle of the night. He slowed down knowing he was close. The adrenaline was starting to wear off as well, and the sheer exhaustion of the last few days fell on him like an avalanche.

Haris knew that even if he showed up to rescue Mitra now, he would be dead within seconds. At his peak health, he wouldn't be any match for an ubir. So he crept forward enough to peek through the trees. He was positioned down river from the island, on the right bank just after the diverged halves of the river reunited. He could see the ubir to the left of the island and the little boat that he had followed heading that way as well. There was something else in the water to the right of the island, maybe another boat.

Embarrassingly enough, it had only taken him thirty minutes or so to get here. That's the furthest they'd gotten in the days of wandering in circles. It was a surprise the ubir hadn't found them sooner. As Haris thought about it, it was possible they had been watching them for days, waiting until they were weak and tired before striking.

Haris had gone back into the woods in search of food. Not too far off, he found a few trees with little fruits that looked something like a warped apple. His stomach took away his common sense and he started devouring the fruit, hoping it wouldn't kill him. The leaves from earlier in the night had only hurt him for a few minutes, but the pain in his stomach had dulled when the adrenaline of losing Mitra caught up.

Now, several hours later, he wasn't dead but was still sopping wet as he munched on the fruit while watching the activities on the island. Not much happened most of the day. The majority of the ubir stayed on the island and it was clear the white-haired one was the leader commanding them.

One thing Haris did notice was that they were restless, pacing back and forth like caged animals. He got minor glimpses of their abilities when that restlessness turned into short brawls that the white-haired one quickly broke up. Something zapped along the ground like electricity, and the water around the island frothed. Trees shifted unnaturally and the skin of one of the ubir shifted colors and textures to look like different animals.

There were a few others besides the white-haired one that looked more...aware. They ordered the others around but ultimately shied away from the leader.

As day turned into night, Haris watched from across the river as the ubir got more and more riled up. Eventually one of them went over to what Haris discovered was a houseboat and emerged with a man. It was hard to see because even the boat was partially shrouded by the trees and shrubs, but he could tell that the man was human and a bit older.

That must be where Mitra is, he thought to himself, looking over the houseboat.

Haris thought he knew what was coming next. He was aware that the ubir killed people as part of a ritual to keep their tattoos intact, but what he wasn't prepared for was the *sport* that they had prior to doing so. Haris was ashamed that he couldn't handle more than five minutes of the man's shouts and screams before he had to go deeper into the woods, away from the sound. It made his heart hammer and adrenaline pick back up knowing that Mitra could be next.

The only thing that gave him a tiny shred of hope was knowing that statistically, the ubir didn't kill more than one person at a time. They spaced them out so as not to waste them. So he had at least a day, maybe more, before they killed again.

Eventually the sound died down and he fell asleep, crouched in a cluster of vines.

THE NEXT MORNING, Mitra woke feeling like she was hit by a bus. She had fallen asleep in the early hours of the morning, after things had quieted down. It seemed even the ubir needed to sleep sometime.

They were startled when the sound of feet hit the deck above. The others didn't look too worried this time and Nick even perked up a bit. It must have meant food and water.

Sure enough, the short, muscular man from the day before shouldered his way in with two buckets; one only half filled with water, and the other with a handful of assorted food items, also not enough. Before he left, he looked at Mitra directly, narrowing frantic eyes at her as if to say, *I'm watching you.*

The remaining five of them dove into the buckets, pulling out slices of bread, rotten apples, a few sticks of carrots and a few slices of deli meat that Mitra had no intentions of eating, no matter how hungry she was. Deli meat sitting out in the Louisiana heat was a no for her.

The water was clean and must have come from a fresh water supply. Ubir would need to eat eventually just like the

Anunnaki did, but where were they getting it? They ate in silence and Mitra found herself curious about the others.

"Where did you all get taken from?" she asked around a bite of carrot.

"I was out for a run by my house a few days ago," Sarah said, gulping down water. "Well, maybe it was more like a week. It was early in the morning and the trail goes pretty close to a creek. I don't even remember it clearly, but I felt a sort of tingling around my body all of a sudden and then I blacked out. Next thing I knew I woke up here."

"That's terrible," Mitra said. "I wonder how they did it."

"They've got magic," Nick said. "I told you. You heard what happened last night. The way the trees were swaying and the river got frothy. That's how they got me too." He swallowed before continuing. "I was out at my parents' house and took the fishing boat in the evening down the water. All of a sudden, a huge wave comes downstream and flips my boat over. I made it to land, but five or six of 'em came out of the trees. One of 'em hit me pretty hard and just like Sarah, I woke up here."

Mitra nodded. "That sounds like what happened to me. But I still don't know what happened to my friend. If he's not here, then maybe he got away." The look on the others' faces told her they thought otherwise. "What about you guys?" she asked the two other women.

"I'll save you the trouble," Nick said with a roll of his eyes. "Rachel was walking home in the middle of the night and was taken by the white-haired dude. She's been here the longest."

At that, Rachel started crying again, muttering, "I'm next, I'm next," into her sleeve. Sarah scooted over and started patting her back and whispering to her gently.

Nick shook his head. "Waste of time trying to make her feel better. She *is* next if you hadn't noticed."

Rachel started crying even harder and Sarah glared at him.

Nick continued, "And the quiet one hasn't said a word other than to pray every time one of us gets picked off. No idea how she got in here. But it doesn't matter how we got here. There is only one door out and it's watched by those things all day. One of us tried to make a run for it last week... they just dumped her body in the river without a second thought."

Mitra thought for a moment. "How many of them are keeping watch?"

Nick and Sarah both looked up at her sharply. "No," Sarah said.

Nick just snorted. "You're dumber than you look if you think you can make it out of here. Remember the part about them having *magic*? They're all rabid as animals and will hurt you just for fun."

Mitra huffed in annoyance. "*How many?*" she asked again.

"Nick is right for once, sweetie," Sarah said. "Don't go looking for trouble. You'll only get hurt."

"We're going to die anyway though, right?" Mitra said. She could understand how afraid they were, but to not even try to escape? Mitra may have been scared senseless, but she wouldn't just lie down and wait for it to happen.

"It's fine, Sarah," Nick said. "Let her get herself killed. As long as she doesn't involve us, I don't care." He turned to Mitra. "The big muscle guy is always close by but there is another that sits up in the tree line, only it rotates who it is. Every time we go out, it's a different person up there. The rest of those people stay on the other side of the island, probably the white-haired dude's orders. The odd thing is, I've never heard them talk. Maybe that's why the government tossed them; they're mute."

Mitra had the urge to shake him but if she hadn't known about the ubir and the Anunnaki, Nick's idea wasn't too bad.

Why else would there be a horde of maniacs with magical abilities running around in the south?

"And what about this boat? Does it actually run?" she asked.

Nick just shook his head and chuckled. "You really have a death wish, don't you? I have no idea if it actually runs, and we haven't heard anyone else come on and it's pretty small...so, no idea."

"Mitra, you can't be serious," Sarah said, eyes wide. "You heard what happened last night, right? That man is dead now. Probably floating in the river. The only hope we have is of the police finding us and getting us out."

Nick barked a laugh. "The police? What do you think they are going to do? You would need to send the entire U.S. Army to stop those guys. Alright, maybe not the entire army, but you would sure need a lot of weapons. And who knows if they can even be killed. On my first day, I saw one of them slash another with a knife right down his arm. A few hours later, when they took us outside, I saw him again and his arm was as good as new."

Rachel had quieted now, having cried herself to sleep. Mitra didn't know how she was going to get out, but once they did, she had no idea how the Anunnaki would handle knowing these humans had seen the ubir.

Mitra spent the rest of the day gathering as much information about the ubir as she could. The only way they were going to escape was if they knew as much about their opponent as they could. There would be two opportunities for them to leave the boat to relieve themselves, but that was it. Mitra spent the time inside drilling the others for information. Only Sarah and Nick were of any help though. The older woman continued her silence and Rachel only woke to cry over her soon-to-be fate before falling back asleep.

"There is one guy that always has a bunch of electricity around him," Nate said, giving in to Mitra's prodding. "Like a wave around him or somethin'."

"And the ugly guy with the water," Sarah said with a wrinkle of her nose.

"Oh yeah," Nick said, raising his eyebrows. "He is pretty ugly. He's the guy who did the magic on the water making my boat flip." He shook his head as if still in disbelief.

"What else? Who else has big abilities?" Mitra asked, mentally taking note of everything they said.

Nick snorted. "You mean besides *all of them*?"

"Well, you know the guy who guards us," Sarah said, pointing toward the ceiling. "I think he does some sort of quicksand thing. Remember I told you one woman tried to escape and her feet just sunk into the ground?" She shuddered. "This is what we are trying to tell you, Mitra. Even if we made it off the boat, we wouldn't make it more than a few feet before they caught us."

Mitra brushed off Sarah's concern. She needed to get off this boat, not only to save her own life, but to find Haris and make sure he didn't die of starvation either. "Who else? Tell me everything you've noticed," she said instead.

Nick sighed in exasperation and started counting off on his finger. "The white-haired dude has the freaky laser eyes, one woman makes the wind go all crazy, I saw one guy's skin literally morph into scales, maybe he's a lizard."

"I'm not sure who, but someone can make you really uncoordinated," Sarah chimed in. "Like your feet go all wobbly."

"What about the woman who came to get...?" Mitra jerked

her thumb toward where their missing member had sat just yesterday.

Nick shrugged. "No idea what she has. Which is why this is a stupid idea. There are a ton of them and five of us, two of which are dead weight."

"Nick!" Sarah exclaimed, glancing at Rachel who, thankfully, was asleep. The older woman just stared off into space. "You don't need to be mean. Besides, Mitra isn't going to actually do anything, right?"

"Nick, hypothetically, do you know how to start this boat?" Mitra asked, eliciting a pointed look from him to Sarah who moaned into her hands.

"Sure, assuming there is gas in it and the key is in the ignition. But, again, the ugly guy will just raise the water again," he said. "You're not very smart, are ya?" he mused.

Mitra glared at him and sat back, allowing the gentle rocking of the boat to coax her mind into action. She mulled over the possibilities of escape. Even if they did manage to take the boat and leave, they would need to find their way out without getting caught again. It was a risk she was willing to take, assuming they could even get that far in the first place.

The five of them munched on their remaining food throughout the morning and rationed the water. No one really talked until it was time for their first break. The boots hit the deck above and started coming down the stairs.

So the big guy doesn't stay in the boat, just nearby, Mitra thought to herself.

The lock on the door jiggled and the door was thrown open. Mitra and the others knew to stand and headed up the stairs with the man following behind. She had to breathe through her mouth to avoid gagging at the stench of unwashed body.

It was a bright morning when then stepped on the upper

deck and Mitra had to squint against the sunlight. To her left, she could see the other ubir on the island, some pacing back and forth, while other stopped to watch the humans come out. It felt like she was a lamb being dangled in front of hungry tigers. They didn't come to hunt her though. She could see the white-haired man among them, and the others never stepped out of line while he was around, according to Nick and Sarah. He always had one or two others with him. Right now, he barely glanced in their direction before turning back to his group.

Mitra and the other humans descended the boat to the little beach and started walking up toward the tree line and then upriver a little further where they were allowed to do their business. As Mitra walked by, one of the trees above them rustled and she looked up sharply. At first, she assumed it was a squirrel, but then she saw two very human looking eyes watching her from the branches. Their owner was a lithe woman who lounged on a flimsy branch. Mitra didn't know how she did that without falling right off.

Mitra must have been walking too slow because the big man grunted and shoved her in the back, causing her to stumble. She was about to turn on him when she saw Sarah and Rachel's wide eyes. Sarah subtly shook her head and Mitra fumed but walked faster.

On their way back to the boat, Mitra was in the back of their group, with the big man behind her again. She was trying to walk as slowly as he would allow so she could get a glimpse of the other ubir.

Suddenly, a form dropped to the ground right in front of her, landing as lightly as a cat. It was the woman from in the trees. Mitra sucked in a breath and stopped with only inches between her and the woman. She was a little shorter than

Mitra with shorn hair and moved as gracefully as a dancer. Something clicked in Mitra's mind.

Basma.

A wolfish smile spread across the woman's face at Mitra's expression. After all their hunting, Basma was here, with this giant pack of ubir. She was here all along. This was the woman that had pushed Kinza off the roof of a building, attempting to kill her. Hot rage clouded Mitra's mind and she raised her arm back without thinking. Before she could swing, an iron fist clamped onto her arm and wrenched her back, nearly pulling her arm out of the socket as she landed in the dirt.

Mitra looked up to see the big man try to shove Basma, but she twisted out of his reached. Their faces contorted and eyes flickered in some unheard conversation. Basma relented and moved back toward the other ubir, but not without shooting one last glance in Mitra's direction. It was a horrid mixture of malice and delight; something she was discovering was a trait of the ubir. She must have known Mitra and Haris had been tracking her.

Mitra got to her feet before the big man could haul her up and rubbed her arm. It hurt but wasn't broken or dislocated. Anger still felt like a hot stone in her stomach as she glared at Basma's retreating form. If she was going to escape, the graceful ubir was one more obstacle she would have to face.

She followed the others, who were white-faced and half expecting her to be dead, back to the boat. When they were below deck again, the man shot Mitra a narrow-eyed glare and she swore he was going to say something, but he slammed and locked the door shut and went back up.

"You're seriously insane," Rachel whispered, not crying for once.

"I need to get out of here," Mitra muttered and sat down to wait for their next break. She didn't tell them that the interaction wasn't unprovoked, and that the ubir woman had tried to kill her best friend.

LATER, in the early evening, the sounds of the ubir picked up and Mitra and the others listened to the sounds of the abilities on the island. The crackling electricity, the howling breeze that came and went, and the shouts of pain and anger as they bickered amongst themselves.

They had drunk all their water and ate the remnants of the food by the time that the big man came back down the stairs. As usual, his erratic movements made the others cower as he lurched the door open, and they filed up the stairs. The sun was on the second half of its arc now and shadows started to form between the trees. Mitra wondered if Haris had found his way back to the truck or if he was lying dead somewhere in the shadows of the forest. She pinched herself to keep from crying at the thought.

As they stepped back down onto the bank, she could see the chaos they had been hearing for the last hour or so. Over the last few days, the ubir had nearly destroyed the island. Trees scorched, the ground upended in places, all the animals long gone. She could see now, some of the trees were on fire in places, and the wind buffeted through the branches. The ubir's normally erratic movements were more dramatic now. They paced and moaned and shouted at one another, lashing out in anger. Even the big man who guided them to their spot in the trees seemed less stable than before.

Some of the ubir came closer than normal and watched them walk by, a hungry look in their eyes. Nick had said they tortured their sacrifices before they killed them. It seemed they were already anticipating the next one and she turned to find silent tears streaming down Rachel's face. The poor girl looked hollow from days and days of crying, but all of their fates were to be the same.

Mitra finished her business first and went to stand off to the side, just barely within sight of the other ubir. She watched them as best as she could through the trees and noticed the white-haired man was not among them. Maybe that was why the ubir were so rowdy? Maybe his authority kept them calmer and in line. They always seemed more focused when he was around.

Mitra felt the hairs on her arm stand up and looked to her left and found the big man watching her openly. He never looked at the others with the same suspicion and it made Mitra uncomfortable. It was like he *knew* that she was planning an escape. She was thankful ubir could only speak telepathically with each other and couldn't read the minds of humans.

Just as the others finished up, she could hear the rumbling sound of a boat engine and knew the white-haired man had come back. Mitra and the group started trudging back to their boat, Nick the only other one who watched the ubir; the other women kept their eyes forward and downcast.

Mitra saw how the leader reacted upon seeing the chaotic behavior of the other ubir. Before the boat had even stopped, he jumped out into the water, shoving other ubir out of the way. He must have been yelling at them because they scattered like wild dogs. They both cowered from and cheered for him.

As the boat came to shore, Mitra could see the few other ubir who were always with him. The last to step off the boat caught her eye. He was young, barely into his teens yet there was an air about him. His hair coiled tightly about his head and his skin was clean. He waited until the boat was fully docked before stepping out, careful not to step into the mud. Compared to the other ubir, his movements seemed...deliberate. He strode up the bank, hands clasped lightly behind his back, as if out for stroll. He looked at the other ubir as he passed them with his head cocked slightly to the side. The other ubir hardly noticed him compared to the leader. Instead of cheering or cowering around him, they all seemed somehow steadier. Like a wave that moved through the group, the shouting, fighting, lurching ubir slowed and focused on the leader as the teen walked among them.

Mitra was forced to look away and up the ramp that led into the houseboat. When they were below deck again and the man had left, Mitra sat down to think. It was only a matter of time before the ubir sacrificed the next person.

Up until now, it had looked like the white-haired man was the leader of the gigantic horde of ubir, but now she was starting to wonder. She didn't know what the teen's ability was, but she remembered Kinza telling her about some of the more invisible abilities some of the Anunnaki had. When Kinza and Zaid were fighting a pack of ubir in Michigan, one of them had a mind-controlling ability and had even forced Zaid to stop breathing. The thought sent shivers down her spine, but what if the teen had the ability to *unite* a group of people; to focus them? Now that she thought about it, the white-haired man left once or twice a day with the teen and a few others, and the remaining ubir on the island became worked up as well. What if, instead of the white-haired man being in control, it was the teen this whole time?

The ubir were distracted with fighting amongst themselves when the teen was gone, but maybe they could use that to their advantage. It would be relatively easy to start a brawl when the leader and the teen were gone, providing the perfect distraction for the humans to escape. Nick said he could drive the boat as well so they wouldn't have to run; they were in no shape for that.

Mitra looked around at her exhausted and terrified companions. There were too many "ifs" to account for and they had no defense against the ubir in the event one of them tried to attack them during the fight. Not to mention, they had no idea how to get back to town. While the others dozed off, she sat there going over every detail she had gathered about the ubir. With her knees up to her chest, she fiddled with the silver chain around her neck, running it back and forth as she thought.

The answer came to her suddenly and she felt like an idiot for not remembering it sooner. A tiny spark of hope spread a small smile across her face as she woke the others to tell them her plan.

CHAPTER 9
NOWHERE TO RUN

"Dang it, Blue! Outta my way!"

Abe stepped over the dog that had tangled itself between his legs as he hurried across his yard. His blood pressure was well past the level his doctor ordered, but he needed to get the old truck up and running. Carrying his box of tools over to the rusted Chevy, he got to work as fast as he could. It was difficult to stay focused when the sheer number of people of people on his property kept growing, reminding him that time was dwindling.

In all his life, there had only been one incident in Abe's life when more than one venari came through his portal. It was back in the seventies and one man had stepped through with a wounded woman leaning on his shoulder; an assignment gone wrong. They had stayed the night in his guest bedroom and were gone before sunrise. It had been enough excitement to last him months. Normally he would only get one of them at a time, maybe carrying a bound, snarling ubir through the portal. The venari themselves were always calm and collected, and never spoke much. It was a far cry from the number of venari that had been stepping through his portal all day, pacing around his house and his lawn, their anxiety palpable despite the lack of chatter.

Abe couldn't help but feel a small sense of pride that it was his call that they had answered. It had taken less than a day for the venari to get here after he sent word out through the Ummanu network. At first, he had doubted they would come, or maybe only a few. Now he was starting to wonder if *all* the venari in the world were raiding his pantry and sharpening their obsidian weapons on his porch. Some he had met before, some he hadn't, and some he hadn't seen in years. One of which was walking over to him now.

Abe wiped a grease-covered hand over his sweaty brow as Savar, head of the venari, strode over to him. The tall, wiry man looked hardly different as he did the first time Abe met him, when he was seventeen. Graying hair at the temples and twin obsidian swords strapped across his back. Abe remembered feeling young and naive before the experienced venari as his father let him through the portal. Now Abe looked older than he did, but he knew appearance meant little when it came to the Anunnaki.

"How close are you?" Savar asked, eyeing the vehicle half as old as Abe was. "I don't want to waste any more time. Every second could be a disaster."

"Just a few more minutes," Abe replied, tightening a bolt. "And you don't need to remind me, people been dyin' and goin' missin' here left and right. I'm the one who made the call, remember?"

The dogs had come running back over at the sight of Savar, but he gave them a stern look and even Blue took the hint and kept his distance. "I don't think this is going to be enough either," Savar said. "There are three vehicles, but we'll need at least twice as much to transport all the venari. Do you have anything else?"

As soon as Savar stepped through the portal with a stream of venari behind him, Abe had called Larry and asked him to close the roads and to leave several county-owned motorboats near the location the bodies were found. The officer had grumbled a bit at the last part, citing that the chief of police would ring his neck without an explanation, but the boats where there within two hours and the roads blocked off. Abe had no idea how Larry would explain that one to his boss, but he had full faith that his old friend wouldn't say a peep about the Anunnaki or the ubir that were using the bayou as their personal hunting grounds.

Savar was right though. Abe looked around at the black-clad venari that kept multiplying. Some carried obsidian swords and spears, others counted arrows and a few polished shields. At the moment, Savar's apprentice, the young man Zaid, who Abe was sure he had seen once or twice, was rallying them into lines and giving out orders. Savar had said Zaid could find the ubir quickly with the information Abe had given them on the location of the ubir, but they needed to get everyone there fast.

Abe looked around at the goods he had collected over the years, lying around on his lawn, trying to decide what could work. There was a half-built go-kart, two sedans missing engines, a lopsided trailer, and in the back of the lot was a forgotten yellow school bus...A gap-toothed smile lit Abe's face.

"I think I've got somethin' for ya."

"Ha!" Haris shouted, finally finding what he was looking for. The stick was more like a skinny branch: sturdy, straight, and with little water weighing it down. A good, proper stick. A stick of warriors. With a grin, he started snapping off the smaller branches and twigs along the side until he had a long pole. Satisfied, he sat down on the wet ground, grabbed the sharp rock he had found, and start sheering off the end of the stick, shaping it to a point. Each stroke brought him a sense of glee, and he was starting to wonder if he was really losing his mind, having slept little the past few days, surviving only on leaves and the little green fruits he had found.

Off to the side, his stockpile of "food" was growing smaller and would only last him another half a day. He had finally run out of options. The night before had rattled him to the core. He knew what the ubir could do to their victims, but hearing it was different. Had he had anything in his stomach at the time, he would have lost it twice over. It was clear he couldn't find a way out of the bayou, and he knew where Mitra was. Haris had decided when he woke up that he would rather die trying to save her than listen to the ubir torture and kill her.

So here he was, sharpening sticks in the trees, hoping the ubir would kill him quickly. He had no illusions of them making it out safely but dying by the hands of the ubir would surely be quicker than dying of starvation. Maybe, just maybe, he could distract them long enough for Mitra to get away, and then *maybe* she would find her way to safety. He figured that would be the best sacrifice he could make in his life.

As he continued sharpening his stick, Haris thought of his mother, which he hadn't truly done in a long time. He wondered what she would think of the man he had become. She had died when he was only sixteen, before he had moved out to Michigan on his own to guard one of the portals. Would she be proud of the little he had done in his life? Thinking of the pragmatic, kind woman his mother had been, he concluded that she would smile and run a hand over his hair at the thought that he was trying to save someone else when he could have easily given up. It brought a sad smile to his own face.

The sun was starting to set now, and Haris wanted to be ready for when the ubir picked their next victim. He could hear them in the distance, he had put some space between him and the river to work, and he swore that they were getting louder.

Giving the stick one last swipe, he held up a rudimentary spear, the tip sharp enough to at least poke an eye out.

"Hang on, Mitra. I'm coming."

"No way. No freaking way. You've lost your dang mind!"

Nick paced back and forth in the small room below deck. Mitra ignored him and continued speaking to the others. "You're going to have to be ready in case any of the ubir come onto the boat. I think they'll be too distracted with fighting each other, but I'm not sure about the guy that watches us."

"You're forgetting the part where he *kills* you first, Mitra," Sarah stressed. Rachel was looking at them wide-eyed and Mitra was sure she would start hyperventilating at any second. The older woman had even glanced at Mitra once or twice as she explained her plan.

"He's not going to," Mitra promised. She hadn't given them specifics of her plan, only what they needed to do when it was time. "I'll knock him out first. We just have to hope that he doesn't wake up before we get the boat running. Nick, you can drive this thing out of here, right?"

"You're an absolute lunatic. They'll kill us all tonight for this." He kept pacing the room, looking out the window. The sun was nearly set and Mitra had heard the motor of the other boat leave nearly twenty minutes ago. She hadn't expected the white-haired man and the teen to leave again so soon, she wasn't mentally ready to enact her plan, but it was now or never. One of them could be sacrificed tonight. She could hear the ubir growing restless and agitated as their shouts drifted through the window.

She couldn't wait any longer. "Just be ready," she said to Nick and got to her feet. She went over to the door that was still locked and started pounding. "Hello! Can someone hear me?! I need to use the bathroom!"

The others gasped and Nick came over and shoved Mitra away from the door. "*What are you doing?*" he hisses.

"I told you, just be ready when I come to get you." She went back to the door and started pounding again, louder this time. "HELLO! BIG GUY! I DRANK TOO MUCH WATER AND NEED A BUSH OR SOMETHING!"

"Oh my god," Nick moaned, shoving his hands into his hair. "We're all going to die."

Rachel started crying again and Mitra pounded even harder, hammering at the door with her fist. Sarah moved to sit with Rachel, her hazel eyes panicked but saying nothing. Mitra kept on pounding. "HELLO! Can anyone hear me? Hello —" She was rewarded with thundering footsteps hitting the upper deck and coming down the stairs.

She backed away from the door just before it was unlocked and nearly thrown from its hinges. The man's eyes were wild and enraged as he took in the room. The others were huddled as far back as they could and only Mitra stood by the door. The man snarled and shoved her back to the wall, grabbing her by the throat, just under her jaw. Panic flooded Mitra's veins and she wondered if this had been a terrible plan after all.

"What do you want?" the man growled, accent thick.

She grabbed his hands, trying to keep him from crushing her windpipe. She could see the unfocused look in his eyes and knew her theory was correct. It had to be the teen keeping them all partially sane.

"I need to use the bathroom...or a bush or whatever," she ground out between breaths.

The man pursed his lips but relented and threw her toward the door. Her shoulder hit the doorframe and she yelped.

"Hurry up," he spat and moved to lock the door behind him.

Before he could shove her again, she scrambled up the steps into the darkening evening. The sky had the barest hint of light left and she had to watch her steps as she went down the ramp to the bank. She barely had her feet on the ground when the man caught up to her and grabbed her arm, practically hauling her along the edge of the river towards the copse of trees that they usually used.

Mitra didn't fight him much, focusing instead on looking for the other ubir. She could see them on the other side of the island, some of whom were already fighting and bickering. It was no wonder that under normal circumstances, the ubir rarely grouped up into more than twos or threes. They used their abilities against each other to provoke one another. Mitra couldn't imagine being that bloodthirsty all the time and briefly wondered if they would have chosen this life again had they known what it would entail. Would they have chosen to stay in Rhapta instead?

The man pulled Mitra along and she looked up into the trees and was relieved that she didn't see Basma, or anyone else, hiding up there. The wind from one of the ubir thrashed through the leaves and made the branches sway violently. It would be difficult for even Basma to hang on up there. The breeze was also a small respite from the oppressive heat of being stuck in that little room all day. The scent of sweat only ever lifted when she was outside for a few moments.

When they got to the trees, Mitra jerked her arm out of the man's grasp and glared daggers at him, hoping he understood how much she despised him.

"Be quick!" he snapped.

She turned and stepped into the trees out of sight. If she took too long, he would come looking for her, privacy was a luxury, so she hurried as fast as she could. She walked in a small circle, toeing the ground with her shoe and felt something rough. Checking over her shoulder and seeing the man hadn't come after her, she bent down and dug out a rock. It was a little bigger than her fist with one pointed end. It wasn't very heavy, but it would have to do. Reaching for her collar, she took a few quick breaths, begging her body for a surge of adrenaline. She didn't have time to psych herself up and only thought about what the ubir had done to the humans, what they would do to *her* if she didn't do this.

Standing up, she shoved the hand with the rock behind her back and walked back toward the ubir. His eyes narrowed upon seeing her with one hand hidden. She stepped up to him. "Give me your hand," he growled reaching for her hidden arm.

Instead, Mitra held out her free hand in a fist. A silver chain was wrapped around her palm and before the ubir had a chance to react, she unclenched her fingers and a small, cloudy white stone dropped, dangling from the chain.

The ubir went down to his knees so fast it was like he was magnetized to the earth. He grunted in pain as he gripped both sides of his head, moaning at a sound Mitra couldn't hear. He was breathing fast and hard and looked like he was fighting it, so without thinking, she raised her arm and smashed the rock over the man's head as hard as she could.

He didn't drop as fast as he did with the Deathstone, swaying for a moment and eyes closing before he crumpled to the ground. When he didn't immediately jump back up, Mitra sighed heavily in relief. The hard part was over. She knelt down and felt at his chest. He was still breathing and he could see the gash on his head already starting to heal, despite the blood that was still leaking out. Looking around, there was no way she would be able to move his body and at the rate he was healing, she wouldn't have much time so she darted back into the trees as quietly as she could.

The sounds of the ubir were close by and she made her way toward them, trying to be as stealthy as a mouse. She put the Deathstone back into her fist, not wanting the sound to alert the ubir and have them come running. She only wanted it ready just in case they came for her. As she got close to the other group of ubir, she could see they had started a few small fires to see by, but they were unattended. They stood in an open clearing by the other side of the small island, bickering among each other.

Finally up close, she could see their faces and shuddered at the maniacal look in their eyes. Most of them were no better than deranged drunks, lashing out at nothing. About twenty feet away, Mitra saw a skinny man who she was sure was the one with the electricity. He was by himself but kept pacing and glaring at a group off to the side.

Aware that every second the big man was healing and could wake up, Mitra stayed hidden within the trees and felt around for a small stone. When she found one, she went and stood behind a wide tree close to the clearing, took a few encouraging breaths and stepped to the side just enough to throw the stone at the skinny man before ducking behind the trunk again.

She heard a soft *thump* as the stone connected with something. Not daring to look out, she listened for something to happen. It was so much harder because the ubir never spoke out loud, but it was only a few moments before something did indeed happen.

A startled gasp tore itself from her throat as a sudden violent wave of electricity rippled across the ground of the clearing in a wave, causing many of the ubir to shout or scream. From her vantage point, Mitra saw the edge of the wave and clenched her jaw in case it hit her, but it never did. Instead, the shouts and screams of the ubir rose in volume and she knew her plan was working.

More shouts and growls and what could only be the sound of crunching bone echoed through the clearing and Mitra chanced a look. The ubir had descended into a full-on brawl across this side of the island. The trees swayed violently, the ground turned to mud in places, the water frothed and rippled, and electricity shot out, lighting up the clearing over and over like when she was little and kept flicking the light switch on and off until her mother snapped at her to stop.

Knowing that the brawl could move into the woods at any second, Mitra turned and ran, hurtling through the trees to the other side of the island toward the boat. She didn't see the big man and assumed he was still where she had left him. When she left the trees, she slowed to a quiet tiptoe up the ramp, trying not to make any noise. The ubir had better hearing than humans, and from the boat, she could see part of the brawl and didn't want to attract any attention. She hurried down the steps and fumbled with the lock on the door. Shoving it open, she was met with four faces that looked at her like she was death itself.

"Time to go," she said. "*Now,*" she insisted, holding the door open.

Despite all his insistence that her plan wasn't going to

work, Nick was the first one to his feet, shoving past her and up the stairs to start the boat. Rachel was still crying but Sarah was easing her up. The older woman at the back wasn't moving though. She wasn't old enough that she needed to be carried but could have easily been a young grandmother.

There isn't time for this, Mitra internally groaned as she knelt before the woman who was staring off into space.

"Hey, lady," Mitra said, not unkindly, "we have to go now. We can't stay here and we have to run when we get to shore so we need to be ready. Can you get up?"

The woman didn't even bother looking at her and just kept staring like Mitra wasn't there.

"*Hey!*" Mitra barked, snapping her fingers. The woman turned to her then, looking affronted. "I am *not* going to die trying to save your ungrateful self. Now *get up!*" she demanded, pulling the woman up by her arms.

The woman mumbled in protest, sounding almost like a whimper so Mitra added, "It'll be okay. We're going to make it," a little gentler this time. Sarah took Rachel by the hand and Mitra helped the woman up the stairs, but Nick came around the corner as they got to the top, face twisted in anger at Mitra.

"What is it?" she asked, worry twisting her empty stomach.

"There's no fuel," Nick hissed at her. "What did I tell you? This stupid plan is going to get us killed. All of those freaks are in a killin' mood and now we have no way to get away," he said, waving his hand toward the ubir who were still fighting across the island. Some of the trees had started on fire again and the ubir were moving closer to this side. They needed to leave right now.

"Then we swim," Mitra said. "We aren't wasting this chance. They are distracted for now; maybe it'll be enough to get away."

Nick muttered something but was already heading down

the ramp, and the others followed. As she was getting off, Mitra saw a bucket off to the side of the deck filled with random junk. In the middle of the pile was a semi-rotted piece of plywood a little larger than her arm. She grabbed it just in case since she had to leave her rock back in the trees.

By the time she got down to the water, Nick was already wading in with Rachel, Sarah, and the other woman close behind. It was full dark now, with only the light of the fires and the waning moon to guide them. As she was about to follow them in, a cold, wet hand grabbed her from behind.

Out of reflex, she turned and sent her fist right into the middle of her assailant's nose, eliciting a low yelp of pain. Mitra immediately gasped when she saw who it was.

"Haris," she breathed, freezing in place. She could see his red hair silhouetted in the firelight, and also the blood gushing out of his nose.

"You broke my nose!" he whispered, rubbing at his face with one hand. In the other was a long, roughly point stick that might've passed for a spear in a child's game.

"What are you doing here?" she whispered back furiously.

"Rescuing you, of course," he replied, looking over her shoulder at the humans getting out of the other side of the river. "But I can see it was bold of me to assume you were the one who needed rescuing."

Mitra was dumbstruck for a moment. Not only was he alive, but he was trying to rescue her, with a *stick*. She wanted to laugh and cry at the same time and settled for shoving his hand aside so she could grab his face and press her lips to his.

When she pulled away, he was grinning, his bloody nose forgotten. "So, what you're saying is that you did miss me?"

A bubble of laughter escaped from Mitra's lips as she looked up at him. In the next moment she saw a huge shadow block out the firelight behind Haris. She shoved him aside so fast, she was sure she gave him whiplash, but right then, the big man Mitra had knocked out was lumbering toward them in a violent rage. Blood from where Mitra had hit him before was caked on the side of his face and head.

Mitra's arm moved of its own accord, swinging the piece of plywood as she released the Deathstone from the grip in her other hand. The ubir flinched at the stone a moment before the plywood connected with his skull in the exact same spot the rock had, and he fell to the ground in a moaning heap.

"You really did a number on this one, huh?" Haris said, staring down at the beaten ubir. Unfortunately, the main pack of fighting ubir had moved close enough that they had heard the Deathstone's cry. Mitra shoved it back into her palm, but it was too late. They had seen them and the other escaping humans.

Mitra dropped the piece of plywood and grabbed Haris's hand. "I think it's really time we left." She yanked him into the water as the ubir shouted and came running across the island toward her. She didn't stay to watch and started paddling across as fast as her arms and legs would allow. As they got close, Sarah shouted to Mitra, pointing at Haris.

"He's with me!" Mitra said as she scrambled up the other bank with Haris right behind her. "Where's Nick?" she asked, pushing the others into the trees. The ubir were in the water now, heading for them like sharks to blood.

"He took off the moment we got to shore," Sarah said bitterly, pulling Rachel along and glancing over her shoulder. "Mitra…"

"I know," Mitra replied. "Just run, I don't have any other plans." The five of them took off through the trees, but they were slow. All of them were exhausted and malnourished. The ubir had the upper hand by far; they didn't need to eat much, were stronger and faster, and had their abilities. Mitra knew in her heart they weren't going to make it. They didn't even know where they were. They ran like rabbits running from blood-thirsty hounds through the dark forest, getting glimpses of the moon between the branches, barely avoiding falling into water again. Rachel and Sarah were both sobbing now as the wind blew around them, electricity zapping across the ground at their heels. Mitra desperately wished she had thought through her plan more as she ran, gripping Haris's hand in her free one. It was too late for that though and she remembered the Death-stone gripped in her hand. It wouldn't do much but maybe it would give the others more time.

Mitra slowed just enough and Haris slowed with her, understanding. The other three women didn't look back as Mitra turned toward the horde that was coming in like a wave through the trees. Not letting herself cry, she squeezed Haris's hand harder, and with one last look at him, stopped and turned, releasing the Deathstone again from her palm.

She thought it would have given her a few extra moments, but electricity so hot it felt cold zapped across her hand the moment she released the stone. Mitra screamed in shocked pain and the dark burn mark that snaked around her hand, dropping the Deathstone into the muck, silenced.

Haris grabbed onto her, pulling her back. She couldn't see his face but felt him tremble as he tried to pull her away from the skinny ubir that stalked toward her, electricity zapping across his knuckles.

The ubir raised his hands and Mitra caught the maniacal glint in his eye and braced herself against Haris's chest.

The first thing she heard was a *thunk*. When she looked at the ubir again, there was something sticking out of his chest, and he looked just as confused as she did. The ubir around him kept coming, two heading for her and Haris, the rest heading for the other women. Suddenly a shadowy blur streaked across her vision and the three ubir in front of her went down. A few more moments and they were dead. Other ubir screamed as a spear sailed from within the trees, only to find its mark in the ubir's chest.

Mitra and Haris stood stunned, huddled against each other as a wave of venari burst through the trees, howling war cries, and moving around the humans like water around stone to clash with the shocked ubir. Abilities flashed in the darkness and cries went up. The blur that had saved them slowed just enough in placed for Mitra to recognize him.

"It's Zaid," Haris said in weary relief, just as Rachel screamed somewhere behind them, "There are more of them!"

In mere moments, a battle between venari and ubir had broken out, with five humans caught in the middle.

CHAPTER 10

BATTLE OF THE BAYOU

Everything came back into focus for Haris when a swipe of claw came too close to Mitra for his comfort. One second, he was convinced he was on death's doorstep, the next he was watching his best friend cut down any ubir that got close. But Zaid had gotten there before the rest of the venari, and one of them got past him. The ubir's hands shifted into the paws—and six-inch claws—of a bear and took a lunge at Mitra, who was digging in the leaves for her Deathstone. Haris panicked and lashed out, jumping at the ubir to keep him away from Mitra's head, and it only got him a slash across his arm as the ubir threw him to the ground. Before the ubir had a chance to come for him again, a venari swept past, imbedding an obsidian sword in the belly of the ubir and then was gone, still fighting.

"Mitra, get up, we have to go!" he said, pulling her to her feet.

"I got it!" she yelled, holding up the Deathstone. All the Anunnaki, ubir and venari alike, in a five-foot radius dropped down, covering their ears, bellowing in pain. Haris snatched the little stone in his fist, allowing the venari to get back to fighting, some of them glaring in his direction. He grabbed Mitra's hand and pulled her through the trees trying to get away from the fighting. It looked like there were nearly as many venari as ubir, but it was hard to tell. The only indicator was the venari were dressed in all black and didn't smell like rotted corpses, but in the dark it wasn't much to go on.

"Wait! We have to get to the others," Mitra said as they stumbled past two Anunnaki, locked in a duel. She pulled him over roots and vines, toward the three women he had seen crossing the river. One of them was hysterical, rooted to the spot, another was crying and trying to get her to move, and a third was looking around in abject horror.

Haris and Mitra made their way through the battle toward them but there were fewer venari over here, most of them concentrated toward the thickest cluster of ubir back toward the river. One of the ubir—the one with scales for skin—was lurching over to the women. Haris watched as Mitra shouted, snatching up a fallen sword and swinging madly at the ubir before it got to the women. The first swing did little more than startle the ubir, and the women. The second swing took the ubir across the chest, sending him to the ground. Mitra's face looked shocked in the near darkness, but she turned to the women and gasped, "Are you okay?"

The shortest one nodded. "Where did the others come from? They are fighting each other now? What was that thing that you—"

"Not now," Mitra said. "We need to get away from the fighting. Come on." She gripped the obsidian sword in one hand and the Deathstone in the other, moving through the trees. Haris ushered the women after her and he brought up the rear, grabbing a fallen spear from the ground. The bottom of it was broken off but the foot-long obsidian tip was still intact. It would do its job.

The ran through the trees, away from the fighting, but the Anunnaki were spreading out. Some of the ubir tried to run as more and more venari came through. The venari were far more organized even though they worked on their own. The ubir thrashed around wildly like cornered animals. The five of them hadn't made it very far when two more ubir came at them from the side.

Haris swung the spear sideways, catching one of the ubir in the cheek. She only hissed at him and tackled him to the ground. Vines burst up from the dirt and wrapped around his throat and legs. One of the women, the hysterical one, started kicking at the ubir but she just shoved the woman away, sending her to the ground as well. The ubir lunged for Haris's throat but then Mitra was there, swinging her dark sword at the ubir woman. They blocked the moonlight, and he could barely see but heard a squelching sound before the vines relented, falling back into the earth.

Mitra reached out a hand, hauling him to his feet and handing him the spear he had dropped. "Don't drop this!" she said quickly and turned to find the women again. Haris saw that she had kept the other ubir back long enough for Zaid to come over and finish him off. He grabbed Haris by the shoulder as he ran by.

"Go that way!" he shouted, pointing off to the right. "There are boats, take one and get out of here."

"We don't know how to get back to town," Haris said, watching the Anunnaki shadows move between the trees. Chaos had unfolded and he couldn't see Mitra.

"There should be somebody waiting for you, but if not, just go and I'll find you!" Zaid was gone before he could reply. Suddenly light illuminated the forest as a gulf of fire erupted in a nearby copse of trees. Orange flames danced in the howling breeze that still swept through the trees. He could see the ubir were already losing the battle and he saw more than a few bodies littering the ground, one of which looked no older than a young teen, eyes open and still.

"*Haris!*" Mitra shrieked and he turned to find another ubir coming toward him, a set of mangled wings hanging from his back. Haris threw his spear at him, lodging itself in the ubir's side and he was surprised that the ubir didn't even try to move. The ubir dropped to his knees and Haris didn't wait to see if he would get back up and ran toward where he heard Mitra's voice. He found her with the three women, huddled between two large trees. Her face was spattered in blood and she was holding her left hand oddly, the right carrying the sword.

Before he could say anything, the youngest woman in the group screamed and pointed off to the side. The four of them turned to see what she was looking at and the shorter woman choked on a cry. Haris and Mitra stepped forward to see better and she gasped right as he saw the body of a blond man lying prone in the muck.

"It's Nick..." one of the women sobbed and even Mitra's face twisted as if she was trying not to cry.

There was no time to mourn the dead though. "Zaid said there are boats this way. Follow me," he said tugging Mitra away from the body.

He led them toward the right side of the battle. More than once, errant arrows or daggers went flying and Haris's stomach dropped at the sound as they whizzed by. The firelight helped them see a bit better and he kept listened for their footsteps behind him. His body had long gone numb from exhaustion, hunger, and adrenaline, and somehow his legs carried him forward.

Just up ahead, he could make out a glint of water in a canal, and sure enough, there were several motorboats with two venari pacing nearby, clearly unhappy at having to wait behind. One held up a hand and a ring of pale light illuminated the space from between his fingers. Upon seeing the terrified faces of the three women, the venari barked, "Come!" and ushered them into one of the boats. An older venari woman was already inside, a full quiver of arrows strapped to her back. She helped them all in and sat at the back of the boat and nocked an arrow while the man got into the driver's seat. Out on the water, the sounds of the battle were dimmer, and the only light came from the man's hand and the half-moon.

Mitra sat on the floor next to Haris as the man wordlessly steered away from shore. It seemed that they were trying to make a quiet getaway so as not to alert the other ubir. Even though Haris's heart was hammering, he felt his muscles relaxing just a fraction; it seemed as though they weren't going to die that night.

Two of the three women were crying, a combination of the shock of the events and seeing their cellmate dead. The third stared wordlessly as the boat pushed through the murky water of the canal, breeze ruffling her grayish hair.

"Are you okay?" he asked Mitra, who sat with the sword in her lap. She hadn't said a word since getting on the boat and they had been going for a few minutes. He could see her better by the light of the venari and he could see her left hand now. Where the ubir's electricity had struck her skin, it had left behind vicious burn marks across the back of her hand and her fingers. "Jeez, Mitra!" he said, grabbing her hand as gently as he could. "Why didn't you say anything?"

She didn't seem to even be in pain as he unwound the silver chain that was wrapped around her palm. He ripped of a piece of his shirt and carefully slipped the Deathstone into the cloth from her palm so as not to hurt the venari. Getting a better look at her hand, he could see the burn marks looked like lightning under all the swelling that had started.

"We need to get you to a doctor," he muttered.

"We need to get me to an IHOP," she muttered back, and Haris couldn't help the grin the spread across his lips.

"Sure thing, babe. You can have as many sugar-filled pancakes as you want," he said, leaning back against the boat. The breeze felt nice in his hair, hopefully carrying the horrific scent away.

"*Babe?*" she said snorting. "I don't think now is the time to—"

A searing *pop* sounded and a second later all the trees on the right side of the canal exploded in quick succession. Someone screamed and Haris pulled Mitra down. He heard the twang of bowstring being released and looked up to see the venari woman firing arrows with a focused intensity. The searing sound came again, and they all shouted as the boat veered to the left, rocking them across the floor. The venari man shouted, ducking down as twin laser beams shot through where his head had been. Haris lifted his head up just enough to see that less than thirty feet behind them, another boat was speeding along with three ubir inside; the white-haired man was standing at the helm, bellowing into the night with every shot missed.

The venari man sped the boat up, shifting the hand forward as far as it could go. It was too dark to see so he had to hold his hand out with the light that emanated from his fingers, which also allowed the ubir to see better as well.

The venari woman shouted, "Hang on!" as if they each didn't already have the boat in a death grip as she fired off arrow after arrow. One of them struck the ubir driving the boat, but the second one immediately took his place.

Haris could see the water rushing past and the silhouette

of the trees on each side of the canal. He was worried that at any moment they would crash into an unseen log. The white-haired man thrashed his head, sending another set of laser beams toward the boat. The venari man ducked again, but not fast enough.

Haris watched as the twin beams struck the right side of his head and his body immediately collapsed back into the water with a splash, his light going with him. The venari woman cried out and grief took over her features for only a moment before she dashed forward and took control of the boat. She was a smaller target for the ubir to hit but she still was in danger of being struck at any moment. The ubir turned on a set of floodlights and Haris swore he saw tears clinging to the venari woman's lashes.

The boat sped forward and Haris knew it was only a matter of time before those lasers hit the hull and they were dead in the water. As if on cue, the whole boat rocked suddenly, and Haris felt water start to spray inside as the lasers carved a deep cut through the side. Water was flooding in and the venari woman steered toward shore and yelled at them to get down.

The boat slowed nearly to a stop as they all ducked down while water gushed inside. Haris's heart was pounding, and he could hear the ubir's boat coming slower as well to inspect its prey. There were no other venari here to save them and they wouldn't make it into the trees before the white-haired man saw them.

Haris looked down at the cloth that he still clutched in his hand. Mitra was pressed into his side, gripping the sword, and he could feel her heart hammering as well. Thinking fast, he caught the eye of the venari woman crouched next to him. She saw what he had in his fist and understood, nodding once in defiance, and slowly and quietly nocking and arrow. She grit her teeth, readying herself for what would happen next.

Haris eased the sword from Mitra's grasp, her eyes going wide and shaking her head from side to side. He gave her a pained look but there was nothing to say, the boat was only a few feet from them and the ubir would be on them in moments. Haris waited until the sound of the boat was so close he couldn't take it anymore.

"Now!" he said, releasing the Deathstone from his fist. The venari woman grunted and he could hear the ubir do so as well as she stood and released a single arrow before dropping down and clamping her hands over her ears.

Haris used every last ounce of adrenaline in his body to haul himself up and with the Deathstone still dangling from its chain, raised the sword, put his foot on the lip of the boat and *jumped*. The ubir's boat had come as close as two feet away and the Deathstone had the two remaining ubir on their knees. Haris had aimed for the white-haired man, screwing his eyes shut and bringing the sword down on his head.

He couldn't see if he had his hit mark as white-hot pain struck his side, his body went cold, and his vision went black.

CHAPTER 11

THE WAY FORWARD

The first thing Haris noticed was the throbbing in his head, followed shortly by the sharp pain in his right side, which was followed by the pain from...everywhere else. He figured that was a good sign he wasn't dead. Or maybe he was dead and death was awful. Either way, he knew that lying there wasn't going to do him any good, so he peeled one eye open first. The light had him squeezing his eyes shut again and moaning. It took him a moment before he could truly open his eyes and he didn't understand his surroundings.

At first, all the colors and shapes blurred together, but as he blinked, everything came into focus and he could see he was in a bedroom, one that he had never been in before. The bed took up most of the room and there was as single window on the opposite wall with dull curtains that looked easily fifty years old and did little to filter out the sunlight that was pouring in. The door was on the left side of the room and to the right, on the other side of the bed, was a giant mound of what looked like junk. Old boxes that hadn't been thrown out, gadgets for the kitchen, and stacks of newspapers. A single chair was wedged in between the mound of junk and the window and its occupant was flipping through a decades-old magazine. The young man, a venari by the looks of his clothes, glanced up and found Haris watching him.

"Ah!" he quipped and got to his feet, the magazine forgotten. "Just wait a moment," he said and left the room, pulling the door shut behind him. Haris wished that he had left him some water, but his throat was too parched to ask for anything at all.

Voices echoed on the other side of the door and he heard a high-pitched bark too. Several pairs of footsteps came down the hall to the door which was shoved open very suddenly to reveal Mitra's rather animated face. Haris couldn't tell if she was angry, impatient, concerned, or relieved, but she came over and sat beside him.

"Finally," she said quietly. "I thought you were about to be stuck in some sort of coma. I would have been so angry with you," she said, her face saying otherwise.

Three other people had filed into the room behind her, taking up what little space there was around the bed. Haris recognized Zaid and Abe—who was smiling ear to ear at him —but he didn't know the third man. He was dressed similarly to Zaid, but was older and wiry, hair graying at his temples. His face looked like he hadn't smiled in centuries either.

"Glad to see you're not dead," Zaid said flatly. He motioned to the unknown man. "Haris, this is my mentor Savar, the leader of the venari." The man gave him a curt nod and Haris moved to speak but found he could do no more than croak.

"Oh, here..." Mitra said, unscrewing a bottle of water she had brought with and bringing it to his lips. He coughed and sputtered a moment but eventually downed the entire bottle.

"How do ya feel?" Abe asked, watching him.

"Like crap," Haris replied.

"You look it too," Zaid said from where he stood with his arms crossed.

"Still better than you," Haris said with a wink that had Zaid smiling. "Now somebody tell me what happened. And where are we?" He felt at his side, the pain blooming around his ribs.

"My guest bedroom," Abe replied, looking around. "This room hasn't seen a guest in a few decades though."

"Well, you know the venari showed up," Zaid started.

"Thanks to the quick thinking of your friend here," Savar said, indicating Abe who stood a little straighter, "he alerted the Ummanu network and got a message to Rhapta when you two didn't come back. We had the venari in-house and in the area all come straight here."

"What happened to the ubir? How did you even find us?" Haris asked a bit incredulously.

"I had a friend fly over and they saw the whole group of 'em," Abe said.

"That, and I could hear the random, giant group of heart-beats from a mile away," Zaid said with a smirk. "It was like a rock concert in the middle of nowhere. We got there just in time it seemed and we took down most of the ubir. Normally we would take them back to Rhapta for a trial, but the circum-stances were unusual."

"A few of the ubir got away, escaping into the woods or the water, but we are already on their trail," Savar said with a frown.

"So I don't need to keep chasing after ubir?" Haris said with a half-laugh as Savar shook his head. "I'm not in the best of shape." Memories from the night of the battle came back. "Speaking of which, what happened to the leader? The one with the white hair? Did I...you know?" He made a cutting motion across his neck.

The group became awkwardly silent and something on

Mitra's face had Haris's heart beating a little faster. She looked reluctant to tell him.

"It's okay," he said, "you can tell me." Could he have hurt someone else as well? He remembered the venari man that was struck down, but had Haris somehow hurt one of the others that were in the boat with him?

Mitra grimaced before reaching over to pat his hand on the bed. She heaved a sigh and looked at him. "You, um, well you jumped over to the other boat, remember?"

He nodded, still confused.

"Well," she continued, glancing at the others, "you didn't exactly make it into the boat. You hit the lip and slipped off, landing on your ribs. And then you just, fell in the water." She had a pained look on her face. "Kisha, the venari who was with us, took your distraction to take down the two ubir."

Haris stared at her, dumbstruck. The others watched him with similar expressions to Mitra, waiting for his reaction. Then, Haris threw back his head and laughed hard enough to send a sharp pain through his ribs. As soon as he started to stop, the thought of him tumbling into the canal had him laughing all over again. A laugh or two may have escaped from Mitra and Abe as well.

Wiping tears from his eyes, he said, "Okay, that hurts," as he grabbed his ribs.

"You'll be fine," Abe said, with a gap-toothed grin. "Just a few fractures."

"How did any of that even happen though?" Haris asked. "I've never heard of ubir coming together like that."

"Mitra figured it out actually," Zaid said. "One of the ubir had an ability that kept them focused, but he's dead now."

"It's bad omen," Savar said, darkly. "It shouldn't be taken lightly. Even though the one with that ability is gone, it doesn't mean there aren't more like him. There are more and more ubir every day and the venari number can hardly keep up. Another incident like this and we could have a much bigger problem on our hands if the human governments find out about us." He glanced at Zaid before continuing, some unheard conversation flowing between them. "We are working on gathering new pupils to strengthen the venari numbers. It may take years before we can start sending more out, but in the meantime, I think we need to make a few changes."

Mitra glanced sharply at Savar, narrowing her eyes.

"It seems," he said reluctantly, "we have been neglecting our human allies. While we will work on gathering new recruits in Rhapta, we are thinking of implementing some changes within the Ummanu, namely, making sure you are all better trained and better equipped. If not to fight the ubir, at least to hold them off until we can get there. I'll speak with the queen, and we'll let you know when the changes are to take place."

Haris nodded. "That's probably a good idea. And the women the ubir captured, what about them? Are they going to be okay?"

Zaid sighed heavily. "They are being held until someone from Rhapta can arrive to wipe their memories. Physically they will be fine, but we can't have them walking around with what they've seen. It should only be a few days. Speaking of which, I need to make a call." He nodded to Haris and stepped out of the room, followed by Savar and Abe, who promised him some lunch when he got up.

Mitra was smiling at him when the door shut.

"What?" he asked, looking her over. Other than the million mosquito bites, she looked far better than the night before. She had showered and changed, which was more than he could have said for himself. The memory of her kissing him came to mind and he had to squash it down for the moment.

"Did you hear what he said? It means the Ummanu are going to be trained! Like real defensive training, and possibly more Deathstone and other weapons. It's so exciting!" she said, grabbing his arm. There was a bandage wrapped around her left hand and the Deathstone was nowhere to be found. He wondered if it was lost in the canal.

"Yes, I heard. I'll be a great warrior soon," he said with a roll of his eyes. "Once I'm better we can head back north, and I'll drop you off before I make my way home."

The smile dropped from her face. "No."

"No?"

"I mean, yes, I need to see my parents, but after that, no." She fiddled with the end of her braid that was bound neatly, the shiny black strands glinting in the sunlight.

"Why?" he asked. The headache was starting to become more insistent, and he knew he would need more food and water soon.

"I know what I want to do with my life now," she replied cryptically.

Haris just raised a brow, imploring her to continue.

She huffed, flicking the braid back. "I want to be Ummanu," she said, staring him square in the face. "I want you to train me."

For the second time since he woke up, Haris's mouth popped open and he stared at her disbelieving. "How exactly do you think that is going to work? Aren't your parents going to have something to say about that?"

"Yes, but I've already thought this through. I'll tell them I got into a college in Michigan."

"But you won't actually be at said college?"

"No."

"Where will you be?" he asked.

"With you," she said as if it were obvious.

Haris's eyebrows went to his hairline at the thought of Mitra living with him. Was that what she had in mind? He had the space but... "I see," he said, mulling it over.

"I'll need you to teach me how to be Ummanu," she continued. "And clearly I need to teach you how to handle a sword better. Seriously Haris, I've never picked up a weapon before but I did just fine. You, however, are beyond terrible. Did you get one hit in?"

Haris had found himself smiling as he replied, "I don't know how I feel about you lying to your parents but I'm game with teaching you everything I know, in exchange for your legendary weapons training." More seriously, he added, "It seems like things are changing anyway. It would be nice to have someone around to talk to."

"Good," she said, with a smile, and the silence stretched on for a few awkward moments.

"So..." Haris prodded, "are you going to kiss me again or—"

"When you're better," she interjected with a roll of her eyes.

"Actually, I'm feeling quite well," Haris said, sitting up on his elbows. "Honestly," he threw back the blanket, "I've never been better."

Mitra's laugh brought out his own and Haris had a feeling he wouldn't be alone anymore.

WHAT?! Kinza said incredulously. Eta was inclined to agree, but she was still trying to piece together the events that had transpired while comparing them to her visions.

They were standing in Kinza's office with Mikah and the other Advisors as Zaid recounted what had happened in the

United States. Eta would write it all down later, but Zaid's retelling only proved the validity of Eta's visions. They had come so close—again—to being found by the humans.

This is twice within a month, Mikah said, echoing her own thoughts. *We need to prepare ourselves for the actuality that we may be discovered sooner than we had planned.*

Kinza had started pacing back and forth in front of her desk, her bright orange dress swishing behind her. She stopped suddenly and turned back to Zaid. *Haris and Mitra...*

Are alright, Zaid said, and the queen's shoulders sagged in relief. *They're a little roughed up, but they'll be just fine. Also...* he turned to Kinza with an awkward expression, *you may want to call Mitra sometime soon for some...updates.*

Kinza gave him a quizzical expression but sighed and nodded. A vision flashed in front of Eta's eyes of a young man and woman sitting in a vehicle, the former grasping the latter's hand and a ridiculous noise coming out of the vehicle. It lasted only a moment but she understood Zaid's meaning and tried to hide her smile.

So no other humans found out? Kinza asked, resuming her pacing. She had started chewing at a fingernail.

Local law enforcement was more than a little shocked by the destruction in the forest, and some people heard a lot of noise that night, but we have friends out there covering it up for us. There were, however, three humans that survived being captured by the ubir. Zaid turned a cautious glance to Mikah, and Eta remembered Mikah telling her they had never gotten along. *I was hoping that you would come back out there and wipe a few minds. I'm not sure how else to clear that one up.*

Mikah's expression was serious and he nodded. *Shouldn't be a problem.*

Great, Zaid said, visibly relieved, *we'll need to leave within the hour.*

I'll go get my things, Mikah said and left the room. The others kept talking for a minute or so and Eta slipped out without their notice. She hurried down the long hall to catch up with Mikah.

Wait! she said when she saw him about to turn down the main hall that bisected the building. *Hold on for a moment,* she said, catching up to him. Physical exertion was not one of her strong suits.

He turned to face her and the mask he usually wore had dropped from his face. He looked nothing less than a child about to receive a long-awaited present.

I wanted to see how you felt about leaving, but I can see you aren't worried about it, she said with a small chuckle. He practically had stars in his eyes and was barely containing his smile.

Worried? No, I'm not worried. I get to see the human cities! Mikah said, gripping her shoulders. Eta could only smile at his delight; she had never seen him like this before. They had been growing closer for weeks and she found this might've been her favorite version of him. It was so unlike the versions of himself that he presented to the world, and for the hundredth time, she was proud she got to see it, if not a little saddened by what caused it. He would only be gone a few days, yet somehow, she felt like she was saying goodbye. How could he want anything to do with her, here in Rhapta, after he'd seen the world? Eta knew what was out there, she had seen it in her visions, but Mikah hadn't. Would he even want to come back after he'd experienced it?

Good, she said, keeping up her smile. *I'm happy for you. Not many people get to leave the city other than the venari.*

You're right, he said, and then remembering, *I'll need to get my tattoo extended, I suppose. This is exciting. I'll need to pack.* He was lost in thought, and Eta didn't want to keep him any longer.

Well, enjoy yourself. I'll take care of your work while you're gone, she said.

He nodded. *Right, I forgot about that, thank you. Okay, enjoy your afternoon,* he said and turned and strode around the corner, still with his delighted eyes.

Eta stood there a moment, an overwhelming feeling of change had barreled through her in the span of an hour. She didn't know if she wanted to cry or scream, but something about the world was starting to feel *different.* She closed her eyes and took a few steadying breaths when she heard footsteps round the corner. She found Mikah coming back toward her. She pulled the smile back into place but dropped it at the look on his face.

I forgot something, he said, stopping in front of her with a mischievous smile. *I wanted to ask you, when I come back,* he said, standing with hands clasped behind his back, *would you like to go on a date with me? A real date. Just you and me. And before you say no, I think we owe it to each other to at least give it a try. If you want nothing to do with me after that, then so be it. But please, Eta, just agree to it this once.*

Heat had risen to her cheeks. Why couldn't her visions have shown her *this?* How could he manage to look so charming yet so open at the same time? But Eta, if anything, was calm and collected. So, raising her chin, she said, *I think I can handle one date, Mikah.*

His smile grew and he nodded. Taking one of her hands in his, he kissed the back of her knuckles and gave her one of his short bows before turning and heading back the way he came. She could have sworn there was a pep in his step that wasn't there before.

Change is coming, indeed, she thought to herself with a smile as she turned and headed deeper into the Grand Hall.

Author's Note

Dear Beloved Reader,

Thank you so much for reading *Corrupt Magic*! I truly hope you enjoyed following along with Mitra and Haris as well as Eta and Mikah. If you did enjoy *Corrupt Magic*, I would be grateful if you would consider leaving a review. Reviews help other readers find my stories, and each review is priceless to me.

Although this book completes the Hidden Prophecy story line, the journey is not over! I'm pleased to introduce the new series *Chronicles of the Rhaptaverse*. The first book is *Rise of the Venari* and it takes place five years after *The Hidden Prophecy*. It shows a new batch of venari as they train to go out into the human world to save humanity from the ubir. Keep turning the pages because I've included a sneak peek of the first couple of chapters as a bonus!

In addition, I've published a novella that is available for free to those who sign up for my mailing list! Portal Magic: A Rhaptaverse Novella is a bridge between *The Hidden Prophecy* and *Chronicles of the Rhaptaverse*. You absolutely don't want to miss it! Download your copy today.

Visit my website (LilySkyy.com) and interact with me on social media. There's awesome merch available for each of my series.

Also, make sure to sign up for my mailing list to be the first to know about new releases and special happenings such as previews and give-a-ways!

I love getting feedback from my readers, and if you'd like to stay in touch (or discuss my books), join me over at the Lily Skyy Readers' Group. I'd also love to connect with you on Instagram, TikTok, and Twitter! Feel free to reach out to me directly via email at social@lilyskyy.com. You may access all of my social media profiles by visiting: https://smartpa.ge/lilyskyy.

Again, I thank you for reading, and I can't wait to join you on the next adventure! Remember, a sneak of *Rise of the Venari* is on the next page!

Sincerely,

Lily Skyy

SNEAK PEEK OF
RISE OF THE VENARI

CHAPTER 1

PREPARATIONS

One-hundred ninety-eight. One-hundred ninety-nine. Two hundred.

Kareem blew out a shaky breath as he pushed through his last push-up, sweat dripping down his face. It was barely half-past six in the morning, and he had already completed his daily exercises, going through the same routine he had done for the last few years.

Sitting up into a kneeling position, he closed his eyes and prepared himself for his morning meditation, the next step in his routine. He tried to focus on the day ahead of him, but kept getting distracted by how nice the breeze felt as it rushed through the trees and over his sweaty skin. The sound of the stream bubbled nearby, tempting him, but he needed to finish his routine. Today was one of the biggest days in his life and he couldn't slip up now; he had been waiting for this for years.

Above him, the unwavering African sun was slowly making its way into the sky, reminding him that he had a little over an hour before he had to be at the house of the venari. Closing his eyes again, he focused on grounding himself, steadying his Aura, and mentally planning out his day.

Up early, are we? came a voice into his mind.

Kareem's eyes snapped open to see his older brother Tejas stepping lightly through the trees toward him. Not a single branch or errant twig clung to his dark clothes like they did Kareem's every time he came out here. He was also lithe compared to Kareem's stockiness; it was hard to believe that Tejas was twelve years his elder.

You know what today is, Kareem replied back into his mind, an ability all Anunnaki had with each other; the ability to communicate through thought. *Today of all days, I can't slip up. I need to be ready.* He closed his eyes again as Tejas sat opposite him with a faint smile on his face.

You? Slip up? I know seasoned warriors who don't have the discipline you do. If Commander Kartik knew a thirteen-year-old boy had more dedication than some of his best men, you would be heading to the warrior's quarter this morning instead of the house of the venari, Tejas said.

Kareem peeked an eye open, catching sight of the city wall far behind him, past the field beyond the edge of the tree line. Even this far out, he could just barely make out the patrols on the wall by the red clothing and paint that adorned all warriors' skin. He snorted and closed his eyes again.

The demand for venari is much higher, Kareem said with hands resting on his knees. *And how can you say that? You're a venari yourself.*

Ah, yes, but I never had a choice. Not like you do, Tejas replied. Kareem opened his eyes again and found his brother leaning back, absently picking at blades of long grass. Up until a few years ago, being venari was practically a shunned occupation and only the unluckiest of the Anunnaki were tapped to join them—which was ironic because Tejas' ability was luck. He had been selected at a young age to join the house of venari and had dedicated his life to hunting down ubir around the world.

With the new queen and all of the changes that had taken place in the great city of Rhapta, being venari had become one of the most coveted positions in the last five years. Not only were the venari under the good eye of the queen, but the job was also dangerous and mysterious, earning someone great admiration and pride from the public. Kareem remembered when he was little, people used to look at Tejas and the dark clothing he wore like he was a ghost or a bad omen, even when Kareem and their family had nothing but the greatest respect for him. Yet now, people smiled at him in the streets, and children begged to hear tales of the human cities and their technology, something few Rhaptans got to see.

Kareem set his brows and said, *Well, my choice is to become a great venari. Mamma and Father think it is a brave choice, and I want to set a good example for Akilah.*

Tejas huffed a laugh. *Akilah is barely seven and her ability hasn't presented itself yet. She has years before she makes a decision. Look, I'm not trying to dissuade you. The venari are needed, and even though the training is brutal, I know you of all people are the most prepared. I just want to make sure you are confident this is what you want. People think all we do is travel the world and collect stories to tell, but Kareem, what we have to do is...hard. Really hard.*

Kareem slid a leg out and leaned sideways, stretching the aching muscles. *I know that, you've told me a million times. This is the right thing to do, though. The ubir are still running rampant and need to be eradicated. Besides, my ability isn't needed elsewhere.* He tried not to scowl.

Kareem remembered how disappointed he had been when, at eleven-years-old, his ability had presented itself to him like a forgotten birthday present. He had set a cup down on the table and it had stuck like the strongest of glues. He had pried and pulled at the cup when, a few minutes later, it had unceremoniously come unstuck and splashed the contents all over his face. Akilah had watched the whole thing, bursting out into laughter at the liquid dribbling onto his clothes. Making things temporarily stick together was not exactly an ability coveted by the venari, but they would take anything these days and Kareem wasn't about to let pride get the better of him.

Well, I'm not going to hold you back, Tejas said, leaning forward to clap a hand on his shoulder. *From what I've seen, things are different now...better. You even get to work in teams instead of alone.*

Kareem nodded, already having gathered every scrap of knowledge about the venari training that he could. Training typically started at fifteen-years-old, but over the years, the venari had changed their ways and allowed younger recruits, giving them several years to train before letting them out on their own. Kareem had heard of a few people at his school who had claimed they would join this year; he wondered if he would see any of them. There were thousands of children in the city, and the house had to start limiting the number of pupils that it took in. Kareem knew the only reason they allowed him and his lackluster ability was because of Tejas. Still, he wouldn't let that dampen his eagerness. You didn't need legendary abilities to be a good venari, and he intended to be the best.

Kareem stretched out the other leg and started on that side, leaning as far down as he could until the muscle felt like it was at its limit. The breeze had switched directions and was now coming from the direction of the city, bringing with it the smell of bakeries and the sound of early morning in Rhapta. Somewhere in the huge city were other pupils just waking and getting ready for the day. Were they in as much anticipation as he was? What would his team be like? How soon would they go out on their first assignments?

He glanced over at his older brother, who had been like a third parent most of his life. *How long until you have to leave again?* Kareem asked, changing the subject.

A few weeks, I think, Tejas replied. *It'll go by fast, though, and before I know it, I'll be lying on a beach in Bali.* He leaned back in the grass, putting his hands behind his head and looking up at the trees. Kareem grinned at his brother's joke. It was true the life of a venari was hard and was no walk on the beach.

What will you do with all of your free time until then? Kareem asked, getting to his feet and stripping down to the loose shorts he wore. He picked his way through the grass toward the stream.

This is and that, Tejas replied. *Ah, that reminds me of why I came out here. I wanted to see if you wanted to get something to eat before you go to the house.* He had closed his eyes and looked serene in the shade.

Sure, Kareem replied, plunging into the water. It was cool and refreshing as he ducked his head under. A thought had him smiling when he came up and spotted Tejas in the same spot. Kareem took a handful of water and chucked it toward his brother.

Kareem's smile wilted when he saw the droplets land everywhere *except* on the now laughing Tejas. He huffed in annoyance and went back to washing himself in the stream.

You should know better by now, little brother, Tejas said, getting to his feet. *And hurry up; I want to see if there are any steamed lemon buns left.*

Kareem scrubbed faster, intending not to be left behind.

Despite being thousands of years old, the city of Rhapta was built on clean lines and straight boulevards that bisected the many plazas. The white limestone buildings were long and flat-topped and did an excellent job of keeping out the heat that was already beating down this morning. Kareem had seen pictures of human cities and was proud of how organized and structured Rhapta was by comparison. It was sectioned into the north, south, east, and west quarters with the central plaza in the center. Two wide boulevards cut through the entire city going perpendicular to each other, each lined with small varieties of baobab trees. It was orderly and magnificent at the same time, rather unlike the cacophonous crowd that had gathered outside one of the food stalls in the central plaza at the moment.

Kareem pursed his lips at the chaos of early morning workers trying to get their breakfast before heading to work. *Tejas, I think you are out of luck for once. There isn't going to be anything left,* he said, looking at the group of people gathered in front of the stall they had decided on. Just then, the stall owner shouted that he was sold out and to come back tomorrow. The group moaned and started to disperse, but Tejas waited patiently for them to leave.

Let's just double-check, Tejas said innocently, hands clasped behind his back.

He just said he's sold out, Kareem said, pointing to the stall owner. *Let's go find something else.*

Just a moment, Kareem, Tejas said, heading up to the owner. *Sir, do you happen to have any steamed lemon buns left?*

The owner gave him a droll look. *I just said I was out, kid.* Tejas was short-statured like Kareem, and it was always funny when people assumed he was much younger than he actually was.

If you could double-check, I would be grateful. Tejas waited patiently.

The owner sighed and turned around, rifling through the cloth-lined baskets at the back of the stall. *Ah—oh!* the owner said, coming back to the front, holding a large white bun. *It looks like I missed one. Lemon, too.*

Tejas thanked the man and paid for the bun before turning back to Kareem with a know-it-all smile. *Looks like my luck is doing just fine,* he said, ripping the bun in half and handing it to Kareem.

Kareem just rolled his eyes and took the piece, lemon custard spilling over onto his fingers. It was hot and he quickly licked it up, enjoying the tart sweetness. Anunnaki didn't need to eat as often as humans, but that didn't stop it from being enjoyable. Tejas liked to indulge much more than Kareem did, but he wasn't going to turn down the offer from his brother.

They wandered around the central plaza until they came to rest on the lip of a long, shallow pool to watch the people coming and going. The plaza itself was huge, with the behemoth that was the Grand Hall sitting on the north side. The remaining three sides were crowded with buildings of business, the library, and swaths of food stalls that came and went each day. The indigo-robed scholars were the most numerous of those rushing at this time of day, carrying books and scrolls with short, quick steps to the library. Kareem also saw a few white-robed Elders speaking with one of the queen's advisors. The advisor's black robes were a stark contrast to the limestone of the buildings, making them stand out like beacons. The only other person dressed so darkly was Tejas, always in his venari clothing. Soon, Kareem would be dressed the same.

Tejas glanced up at the sun. *It's almost time, do you need help gathering your things?*

Kareem shook his head. *No, I want to do it myself. I have*

everything packed anyway. I just need to say goodbye to Mamma, Father, and Akilah.

All right, Tejas said with a proud smile, *I've got a few things to do today, but I'll probably see you around the house. Good luck, Kareem.* He rubbed a hand over Kareem's short hair and headed off toward the west side of the plaza.

Kareem took a steadying breath. He had wanted this for years and had been preparing for almost as long. He knew everything there was to know about the venari and trained himself physically and mentally daily. The next step was just to arrive.

He could do this.

THE HOUSE OF THE VENARI

The side streets just off the east side of the central plaza were much quieter, with only a few people coming and going. The buildings on this street were long and low, only two stories at most. Kareem already knew the house of the venari was the one without windows. A set of large, wooden double doors stood forebodingly at the front with no sign or indication that the city's venari lived and trained here. Kareem eagerly hiked his bag further up his shoulder and knocked three times. He thought he could hear the faint sound of people training coming from the roof, but he couldn't be sure.

The door opened quickly to reveal a broad man with arms as thick as an ox. Before he had a chance to say anything, Kareem interjected.

Hello, my name is Kareem Maamoum. I'm one of the new venari pupils and I'm to start training today. I'm supposed to arrive by half past seven, and here I am. He adjusted the strap digging into his shoulder.

The big man raised an eyebrow. *Well, Kareem Maamoum,*

new venari pupil, you might as well come in. He moved to the side, allowing Kareem to see into the darkness beyond.

Kareem nodded his thanks and stepped inside, immediately getting a whiff of sweat and...mint? As he moved inside, he quickly discovered what he had heard *were* the sounds of training, but they weren't coming from the roof. There was a short dark hallway that opened up to the center of the building where daylight illuminated the center space like they were at the bottom of a deep well. In the middle sat a massive open-air training ring filled with sand, the sunlight and fresh air coming in from above. Inside were many pupils and full-fledged venari locked in combat of various styles. Kareem looked around in wonder. He had heard about the house of the venari many times but was never allowed inside.

There were two levels, both open to the training ring, with many doors on each floor. Kareem could see dark hallways extending off in-between a few of the doors, leading deeper into the north and south wings of the building. Despite the outside of the building being built with the same white limestone as the rest of the city, the interior of the house was lined with dark wood floors, railings, and staircases along the hallways. The venari themselves wore the same dark human clothing as Tejas, almost utilitarian in style. The pupils, however, had on gray training uniforms. The loose clothing that tightened around shins and forearms made it harder for the fabric to get in the way and slip around during combat while still giving the wearer flexibility. Within the groups fighting in the ring, the dark-clothed venari were clearly the better fighters, their movements precise and quick compared to their bumbling, gray-clothed counterparts.

From where he stood, Kareem could see a few other pupils that wore neither the dark nor gray clothing of the venari or pupils. He knew there were nearly twenty new recruits this year that were all moving in today as well. Some of them lounged confidently against the railing on the upper floor, watching the activities in the ring, while others stayed in the shadow, hurrying to find where they needed to be.

Your room is this way, young one, the big man said, indicating a narrow wooden staircase to the left. He began telling Kareem about the house as he marched up the stairs, Kareem right behind him. *Boys' rooms are in the north wing and girls' rooms in the south. You saw the main training ring in the center and most of the rooms surrounding it are offices or classrooms. You'll receive your schedule later this evening after Savar's introductions. While you are here, you will give respect to the venari; if they tell you to do something, you do it. Other than that, there are not many rules. Savar believes in natural consequences as much as possible, unless you put someone else in danger. With that being said, there are no restrictions on using your ability, but be warned, if you harm another unjustly, the consequences are extensive.*

Kareem had to restrain himself from mentioning that he didn't need that speech. It's not like he could stick someone to a chair to death. His ability wore off within minutes. *Yes, sir,* he said anyway. They had followed the upper walkway halfway around the training ring before turning left down one of the dark halls that led deeper into the north wing, where he got another whiff of the mint scent. In here, blue Aurastones sat at intervals along the walls to light the way. Aurastones—their true name was Magalkan'a—were revered all over the city, and it was believed that the Anunnaki's abilities came from the large deposit that Rhapta sat on for the last several thousand years. They were a comforting presence all around the city, always emitting a faint blue light.

They passed several doors without stopping, taking a few turns here and there. Kareem hoped he would remember how to find his room in the maze of dim hallways. They eventually came to an area where mostly gray-clad pupils wandered about, and the big man stopped before an open door on the right.

Here is your room, I'm not sure where your roommate has gone off to, but you'll meet him soon, he said. *Savar will be giving a speech in—*

In fifteen minutes, Kareem said, stepping inside. *I know; I read the letter that was sent to me with the first day's instructions. I'm sure I can find my way back.*

The big man exhaled. *All right then, good luck, and don't die.* He went back the way they came.

Kareem wondered how likely it was that he would really die, especially during training. The thought was quickly replaced by his inspection of the room. It was small at best, with four walls, no windows, and plain furniture. There were two beds, two desks, and two shelves for clothing. One side of the room was already filled with bedding, clothing, and a few small bags. The shelf had a stack of books and scrolls as well. Kareem nodded in approval. Pupils were told to bring minimal items since they wouldn't need much during training. The life of the venari was not one of luxury, and material items were mostly related to their needs on an assignment.

Placing his single bag on the empty bed relieved the building tension in his shoulder. He had brought nothing but the bare necessities. He did have a few beloved books and knickknacks, but he left those with his parents. They didn't mind keeping his extra things in case he wanted them in the future. His mother had been a tearful mess when he had gone to say goodbye. It wasn't a true goodbye, though; he was just living on the other side of the city. Even Akilah had understood he wasn't really going away, only starting a new chapter in his life.

As he was untying his bag, he heard a sound at the door. He

turned to find a kid roughly the same age as Kareem standing there with a scrunched expression. He was looking around at Kareem and the bag he had placed on the bed. In his hands was a large book.

Kareem brightened. *Hello, you must be my roommate,* he said as the boy walked into the room without greeting.

Yes, hello, I'm Ovi, the boy said, heading over to his bookshelf, no longer making eye contact.

Well, it's nice to meet you, Kareem said holding out his hand.

The boy flinched back away from him. *I don't like to be touched. Sorry,* he said, turning back to his bookshelf to place the large volume next to the others. He didn't say anything else, so Kareem dropped his hand. Maybe he was shy?

Not wanting to bother him, Kareem went back to his bag while Ovi went through his own items. It wouldn't take long for Kareem to unpack, and he still had a few minutes before he needed to head to the training ring, anyway. He was itching to see the rest of the large building and didn't want to get lost in the future.

Hey, he said, turning around. *Do you want to go look around a bit? Maybe get the lay of the land?*

Ovi turned to look at him over his shoulder from his hunched position on the floor. *No way. Savar's speech is in ten minutes; I can't be late,* he said, looking almost annoyed that Kareem had asked. He turned back around without waiting for an answer.

Kareem internally sighed but only shrugged his shoulders. He might need to work on getting his roommate to open up a bit. In the meantime, he wanted to get a head start on anything he could, so he left his half-unpacked bag on the bed and headed out into the hall.

He initially turned right but quickly got turned around and had to head back left. All of the doors were identical as he walked this section of the north wing. After a minute of wandering, he realized the halls were set up in a cloverleaf design with several dead ends and only a few halls that actually led back out. He only discovered this by following the trail of people coming in and out. He nodded and said hello to those in passing, noting the different abilities he saw. Many had the flashy elemental abilities of wind or water, while others' skin and features shifted at will. Kareem knew that many abilities were not seen by the eye, much like his own, but it was still interesting to watch the conspicuous ones. As he got closer to the venari rooms, he saw a black-clad man stride past him, trailing mist behind. As the man turned the corner, the mist flicked around the corner with him like a cat scampering after its master.

It didn't take long to get back to the main walkway that looked down over the training ring. There were a few people gathered there, but it didn't look like anything was starting yet, so Kareem kept going toward the south wing. As he passed the rooms by the training ring, he peeked in, spotting worn desks and chairs, books and scrolls, and a few older venari setting up. *These must be some of the classrooms,* Kareem thought as he moved on to another hallway leading deeper to the south wing.

This side of the building looked much like the other half, a cloverleaf design of rooms with identical doors. Some were open, others closed, and everything was just as sparse with the lingering scent of mint. As he turned to head back, he saw a group of girls standing off to the side. One of them was holding her hands out, palms up for the others to see. Kareem thought he saw the air practically ripple in waves above her hands. He didn't know what it was supposed to do, but the others hummed in appreciation, smiling at the girl.

Kareem was so absorbed in watching the ripples that he

suddenly found himself colliding with a wall of bags hard enough to knock both him and the unsuspecting bags to the ground. It took him a moment to realize what had happened before he struggled to sit up. He was unharmed but a little confused. The group of girls shrieked with laughter as he got to his feet, and he realized it wasn't a wall of bags but a man carrying way too many at once. He looked terrified as he quickly set to picking them all up.

I am so sorry— Kareem started to say as he reached for the bags.

You should be! came a shrill voice in his head. *Is there something wrong with your eyes?* The voice came from a girl standing behind the man. She was slightly taller than Kareem with scornful eyes as she looked down at him. Her waist-length hair was set into many shiny twists that she swung behind her shoulder. His immediate thought was how impractical they were for a venari.

I said I was sorry, he stated hotly. *Is this your father?*

The girl gave a faint scoff. *This is our serving man,* she said. *I pay him good money to carry my bags safely. And now you've kept him from doing his job.*

Zara, one of the girls from the group to the side, called. Her hair was shorn almost to her scalp. *Leave the poor boy alone. His family obviously has never had a serving man before.* The group giggled as they looked Kareem over.

Zara stood in front of him imperiously as if he was the one blocking her path and not the other way around. The man had gathered nearly all the bags into his arms again and set off down the hall.

That's no excuse, Zara said. *Those bags are expensive.* Kareem was annoyed when she gave him a sardonic smile, the full apples of her cheeks rising under her eyes.

Are all of those really necessary? Kareem asked, watching the man struggle down the hall, teetering under the weight. *We were only supposed to bring the basic necessities.* He assumed it was her first day as well since she was dressed in neither venari darks nor pupil grays.

Who are you to tell me what is necessary? she said, her voice like ice. Kareem could have sworn the hall actually cooled just then.

If you want to be a good venari—

Then I wouldn't be asking you for advice. She gave him one last look like she was inviting him to say something and then brushed past him down the hall. Kareem turned to watch her go, incredulous at her rudeness. Shaking his head, he went back the way he was heading, the group of girls giggling again as he went by.

As he got close to the main walkway again, he realized the new pupils were filing down to the training grounds, with many of the venari lingering on the upper floor around the railing. Putting the rude girl out of his mind, Kareem hurried down the staircase to the sand below, finding himself a spot in the middle. Thankfully, nothing had started yet.

The group was facing toward the back of the ring, and he could see why. Standing up front were several men and a few women, most of which were now household names among the Anunnaki. The oldest man stood in the middle. Tall and wiry, Savar Basu had been the leader of the venari for decades, though he hardly looked like he was in his sixties. He stood with a ramrod-straight posture, surveying the new pupils that were entering. To his right stood the only other man more well-known than Savar. Zaid Hatem was known in every circle in the city, and not just for being Savar's apprentice and future head of the venari. He was also the queen's consort. Kareem spotted a few girls in front of him trying shamefully to make eye contact with Zaid, who looked almost as austere as Savar.

The last person of note was behind Savar to his left. A muscular woman stood with arms crossed while two other venari leaned against the railing behind her. A dark hood hid her features in shadows, but Kareem knew it was Hessa Darvish. She was a few years younger than Tejas but had risen among the venari quickly by bringing in nearly double the ubir that most venari did, and without a scratch on her. Kareem remembered a few of his classmates claiming that she was a literal goddess. Even amongst the venari, she was spoken of in awe.

Thank you all for assembling so quickly today, Savar started abruptly. His voice was quiet but firm in the minds of the pupils, commanding them to be silent. The crowd quieted down and Kareem turned to see Zara just now entering the ring with two other girls beside her. They settled in at the back of the group.

My name is Savar and many of you will know me as the long-standing head of the venari. You will get to know me and the other trainers very well in the coming months and hopefully years, he continued. *You've all been given short instructions on what today entails, but I will now divulge what will happen going forward. You've all either been tapped or have chosen of your own free will to join the venari ranks. In the past five years, our number has tripled due to some sort of popularity.* Savar glanced briefly at Zaid before continuing. *We've updated our approach to training, but it will be difficult to say the least. If you think you will come out of training unscathed, this is your chance to leave.*

He paused, waiting to see if any pupils took him up on the offer. None did.

You all know the sole purpose of the venari is to hunt down, capture, and return the ubir to Rhapta. The venari are truly humanity's first protectors against the ubir, and by extension, our first protectors against humanity. The life of a venari is harsh and unforgiving. Your life will be devoted to the cause, and you may be away from the city and your families for long periods of time. What you have to do on those assignments will be even harder. The ubir were all Anunnaki once. Mothers, cousins, and brothers, all of which have gone mad and now practice the blood rite. Remember that. When you are out there hunting down ubir, you are bringing back someone's family to be executed.

The room had gone deadly quiet. Savar's words weren't unknown but hearing them was sobering.

As far as your training, he continued, *it may take several years before you are allowed to graduate to a full venari. You will each have a partner for the duration of your training, and potentially your life as venari. You've already met them; your roommates will be your partners.*

Kareem internally sighed.

In addition, throughout training you will be placed in teams of four, and each team will have a venari mentor. There will be trials to complete as a team as well as in pairs. The venari rarely work alone now, so learning to work as a group cohesively will be your main focus. You need to rely on each other's strengths and balance out your weaknesses. When you are out in the world, you will only have each other. If one of you falls, you all fall. I expect that some of you will not even make it through training. You will graduate into full venari when you complete three unsupervised assignments and have your mentor's approval that you are ready. Some of you will be ready sooner than others, but you will not graduate until your entire team is ready. So, focus on building each other up instead of only yourselves.

Excitement was building in Kareem, making his fingers drum on his pant leg. He intended to graduate in record time, so his team had better be ready. He shuffled from foot to foot, eager to begin.

Savar took a breath, glancing around the room. *Now, we'll sort you into groups and assign mentors. We will have a prelimi-*

nary exam shortly. After that, you are freed for lunch and then the classes begin in the afternoon. The real work begins tomorrow, though. He turned and nodded to Zaid, who pulled out a piece of paper and stepped forward.

An exam? Kareem thought. He hadn't heard about an exam on the first day. He hadn't prepared for that at all. What could they be testing them on? Venari history?

The following pairs will become teams, Zaid called, reading from the list in a deep voice. *Caden El Tain and Idris Lajami will be paired with Faiza Shahd and Inaam Kirdar.*

Kareem heard a few boys groan.

Zaid went down the list. There was a total of five teams with one team being short a person. Apparently "fair" was not a term known within the venari. Finally, Kareem heard his own name called.

Kareem Maamoum and Ovi Fadel will be paired with...Zara al-Hazmi and Benita Chudasama.

Kareem wanted to scream. The chances of there being more than one Zara were slim. He turned around and sure enough, Zara was glaring daggers down her haughty nose. Exhaling hard, he turned back toward the front.

Zaid had folded up his paper. *If everyone could find their teams and get together, your mentor will be with you in a moment. They will give you more details on what is to come next and what will be expected of you in the coming months.*

The group moved, people coming together to find their teammates. Kareem had started the day feeling so confident and prepared. Could he really not graduate until the entire team was deemed worthy? There had to be some way out of this. Zara looked like she would be one of the first to drop out, and Ovi wasn't a good sign so far.

Focus, Kareem! he berated himself. There was no way he was going to do this with that sort of attitude. There had to be some way through this. Even if his teammates failed to do their part, the trainers would have to see that he was fit enough to be venari. He would make sure of it.

Unclenching his fists, he went to find his team.

Want more of Rise of the Venari? Visit my Amazon author page to grab it!